AWAKENED BY THE SHEIKH

DESERT KINGS, BOOK 4

DIANA FRASER

BAY BOOKS

Awakened by the Sheikh
by Diana Fraser

© 2015 Diana Fraser
Print Edition
ISBN 978-1927323137

Cara Devlin's sexy voice lands her the job as translator to the King of Ma'in with a salary that will ensure she can leave Ma'in, and the painful memories of a husband who used her, and start afresh. King Tariq is devoted to his children, his country and remaining single. He soon realizes Cara could prove useful in his business negotiations... but only providing she doesn't know she's being used.

—Desert Kings—
Wanted: A Wife for the Sheikh
The Sheikh's Bargain Bride
The Sheikh's Lost Lover
Awakened by the Sheikh
Claimed by the Sheikh
Wanted: A Baby by the Sheikh

Print Edition

For more information about this author, visit:
http://www.dianafraser.net

This is a work of fiction. Names, characters, places, and incidents are the product of the author's imagination, and are used fictitiously. Any resemblance to actual events, locales or persons, living or dead, is co-incidental. All rights reserved. Except as permitted under the US Copyright Act of 1976, no part of this publication may be reproduced, distributed or transmitted in any form or by any means, or stored in a database or retrieval system, without prior permission of the author.

❋ Created with Vellum

PROLOGUE

"Sahmir, don't let me down. With Daidan in Finland, it's up to *you* to make sure the French consortium are willing to come in on the deal." King Tariq ibn Saleh al-Fulan signed the last of the paperwork and signaled his assistant to leave. He looked up at his brother who was apparently absorbed by a television advertisement. "Sahmir! Have you been listening to a thing I've been saying?"

The only response was an upheld hand while Sahmir remained entranced by whatever he was watching.

Tariq sighed. He must have been mad to entrust such a delicate mission to his dilettante brother. But what choice did he have? With his other brother immersed in the diamond industry in Finland, there was no one else he could trust and he was needed here.

He jumped up and stood, hands on white-robed hips, looking out at his city's high-rise towers that shone blood-red in the setting sun. He couldn't help feeling the familiar acrid burn of bitterness on his tongue. Like most things appearances were deceptive. When he looked at his apparently prosperous city all he saw was the debt his father's avarice had laid upon his country. He turned his back to the view. "Sahmir!"

Sahmir looked up at him distractedly. "What? Oh, don't worry, I have it sorted." He grinned, with the easy confidence of an indulged youngest child. Tariq shook his head. His brother could charm women from their husbands, extract money from the wiliest investor, could coax desert flowers into bloom if he'd been of a mind, and he'd always been able to twist his family around his little finger.

"I hope so—the future of our country depends on it."

"I'll get the money and you deal with the Aurus board."

"I wish it was simply a matter of negotiation—*that* I can deal with—but we're beyond that now. They want the contract renewed for another thirty years, or the money. And I'm just going to have to stall them until you secure the funds."

"Come on, Tariq. You'll be fine. You always manage to get your own way. That's why people call you a *wahs*—a brute!"

"So long as I gain control of our country's finances once more, they can call me what they like."

Sahmir stood up and stretched. "Don't worry, I'll come up with the rest of the cash—I'll play my part, you play yours. My focus is complete, dear brother." His gaze drifted back to the screen which showed a river of chocolate pouring into a giant wrapping, branded with a household name. "Almost complete. It would take a saint not to be distracted by this." He pointed to the television. "Listen to the voiceover."

Tariq glanced at it. "It's an advertisement. Unless it's advertising a way in which to regain control of a country's finances, I really have no interest."

"This, dear brother, isn't just any advertisement. Listen."

He increased the volume and a feminine voice—sexy, velvety and alluring—purred from the speakers. Tariq stopped dead in his tracks. The voice conjured up intimate moments, whispered secrets, the heat of closely pressed bodies... The voice stopped and the advert changed. Sahmir turned off the TV. "Gorgeous voice, hasn't she?"

Tariq had to agree. He turned back to his brother. "Who is she?"

Sahmir beckoned over a maid to re-fill his coffee cup. "I don't know. And unfortunately, my brother and king is sending me to Paris for the foreseeable future so I won't be able to find out. But I can't resist tuning in to hear her. Why? Are you interested?"

Tariq huffed dismissively and looked down back at his papers. "Don't be ridiculous."

"Seriously. You should find someone like that—someone sexy and beautiful—to give you some light relief."

"The last thing my children need is for me to parade sundry women before them. They need a steadying influence since Laiha died."

"And *you* need *fun*. If you don't want to have a woman in front of your children, why not take one away with you, to the meeting at Qusayr Zarqa? Use our desert castle to impress not only the Aurus Group, but also a beautiful young woman."

Tariq sighed again. "I'll be *working*, Sahmir. *Work*, remember? It's when you don't have fun, but discuss business with people. It's serious. Like *you* should be about what you have to accomplish in Paris over the next few days. I can't do anything with the Aurus board until you get the French consortium's agreement in writing and the additional cash. If the two of us work together, we can pull this off. You should be taking this far more seriously."

"I always take everything seriously, including women." Sahmir laughed and set down his coffee cup. "Come on Tariq, loosen up. This deal's practically sewn up. The French are keen to be the minor shareholder on any gold mining venture we choose. You just have to keep the Aurus Group sweet until I get the deal signed and sealed. After that you can enjoy yourself in the desert with the mystery woman with the beautiful voice for a few days."

Tariq gazed out to the city of mirrors and towers from which the sun's rays had now disappeared, replaced by the strident false light of electricity, so hard won by his country. It shimmered before him like the mirage of security and wealth that it was. "I can't rest until the deal's signed." He turned to Sahmir. "Anyway, you should be going."

"Sure." Sahmir looked at him with a strange expression of smug satisfaction on his face, as if he'd thought of a good idea. He pulled out his phone, entered a few digits and brought it to his ear.

Tariq narrowed his gaze. "And don't get any ideas about broaching the subject of gambling, here in Ma'in. I'll not have it."

"Would I do anything like that?"

"*Yes*, you would."

Sahmir nodded thoughtfully. "Yes, I suppose I would. But you can trust me on *that* point."

Years of living with his charming, but feckless, younger brother had taught Tariq to be suspicious. "Does that mean there's a point I *can't* trust you on?"

Sahmir grinned. "You go. Half the palace is waiting for you."

Tariq nodded, accustomed to the burden of a country's future on his shoulders. "The Aurus people will be arriving in a week. Let me know as soon as the Paris deal's signed."

The last thing Tariq saw as he left his study was Sahmir,

talking on the phone, the grin still lurking in the corners of his mouth. Tariq didn't have time to argue with Sahmir. Whatever he was up to, no doubt Tariq would find out eventually. So long as it didn't affect the outcome of the next few weeks, it didn't matter. Nothing else mattered other than the future of his country.

CHAPTER 1

One week later

"I've already told you, I'm here to see the King."

Cara Devlin was irked when the Palace Guard barked out a short laugh of disbelief, and she turned to the other one for support, but all she met was another pair of brown eyes, narrowed with amusement. He cleared his throat as he tried to control his laughter.

"Of course, miss. And you can show us no written papers confirming this. All you had is a phone call... so you *say*."

Again, the exchange of knowing looks. Did they think she was some kind of palace groupie? "That's right. I was to report to the palace at four pm. And here I am."

"And here you are," one of the guards repeated, his slow drawl indicating more precisely how unimpressed with her presence he was than any words could. "And here you'll *stay*. We've an important function this evening, so if you'd go and wait over there in the lobby, I'm *sure* the King will make time for you as soon as he can."

Cara gripped her laptop and suitcase more firmly and

stood as tall as her five feet two inches allowed. "I've already told you. This was a last minute arrangement made by Prince Sahmir to my agency for my services as a translator for a series of meetings over a week. I have no paperwork beyond that. Why not check with the King's office?"

One of them glanced at her again. He seemed no more impressed than the first time. "Sure, when we get time. Now move along please."

This was ridiculous. She'd leave. She turned around and walked past the group of foreign businessmen with whom she was meant to be working, who were being ushered inside the palace without any questions. They didn't give her a second glance. She was as invisible as ever, utterly lacking the glamor of wealth, power and good looks that these people radiated.

Good looks and power she could do without. But money, she needed.

She heaved a frustrated sigh. She had no choice, she couldn't just leave. With debts incurred from when her father had been sick, and a husband who'd taken what few assets she'd possessed, she needed more money than translations and voice-overs could raise so she could start afresh—a new life in a new country.

She gritted her teeth. Just a week's work and then she could leave this country of failed dreams forever. Suddenly she remembered something the agency had mentioned. She turned around and retraced her steps down the path lined with towering palms, toward the columned portico of the palace.

"I told you to wait, miss."

"And I told *you* I've been asked to come here. If you don't believe me, go tell the King I'm the voice from the chocolate ad." Their eyes narrowed with attention. "Hazelnut cream to be precise." She cleared her throat. "'The sensuous slide of

cream on the tongue and down the throat, the promise of—'"
She stopped reciting her lines the moment the guards registered who she was. Their attitude changed instantly. The elder guard snapped his fingers and the other guard disappeared into the palace. It was only a few moments before a harried-looking Palace official arrived to escort her inside.

She followed the man into the palace. Their footsteps echoed on the marble floor as they entered a large reception area, all cream and gold opulence. The walls soared up two stories high, with each story framed by a series of gold-trimmed balconies. The area was empty of seating and tables, designed to impress with its austere glamor. She'd heard of the riches within the palace but had never been inside before. The capital city of Ma'in was built on the wealth of the gold discovered nearly thirty years before and all its buildings were new and impressive. But not on this scale. Despite that, Cara felt disappointed. The palace could have been in any city, anywhere in the world. Ma'in was steeped in a rich history her father had spent his life studying. But there was no sign of it here.

The official opened a reception room and ushered Cara inside but when she turned to speak to him, he'd vanished. She felt uncertain, as she saw the men talking at the front of the room beyond the highly polished mahogany tables. A servant approached and offered her a coffee. Eagerly, she dropped her laptop and suitcase and accepted it. She sipped the strong coffee appreciatively as she looked around. Usually, she was hidden away in a translator booth at conference centers, not seated with the conference participants. But here she was seated with them. Although she was under no illusion that would make her more visible.

She glanced around at the three men—two Japanese and one from either Portugal or Brazil by the sound of it, but no one from Ma'in. At that moment, the large double-entry doors opened slowly and Ma'inese officials dressed in traditional robes walked in and greeted the others. As the men exchanged formal pleasantries, all oblivious to her presence, she scanned their faces, trying to identify which one was the King. However there was no sign of him. She walked over to the window from which she could see a lush courtyard, trimmed and clipped to within an inch of its life, but still refreshing after such bright opulent austerity. Then she saw him.

He stood at the window of a room across the courtyard from her, doing as she was doing, looking out at the greenery while he was on the phone. He was tall and broad-shouldered, swathed in white robes that shone brightly in the sun that streamed through floor to ceiling windows. He turned suddenly and she saw his face and felt a jolt of recognition. She knew his features from countless media appearances but had never seen him in person. He'd always been described in terms of awe and majesty—less of the handsome and more of the ruthless, uncompromising sheikh. She could see how he'd acquired those epithets, but the descriptions had entirely missed his magnetism.

He was talking on the phone, unsmiling, his eyes dark and intense, a frown pressing onto his brow. She took another sip of coffee and then he suddenly looked up and met her gaze. A wave of hard hot adrenalin shot through her. She felt as if she'd been discovered, not just noticed but really *seen*. His eyes didn't shift from hers and despite her brain ineffectually telling her she should move, do something, anything, she remained rooted to the spot, as the adrenalin conjured up a heat that swirled mercilessly around her body, like a desert wind unsettling sands which had long been still.

Then the maelstrom glance turned away and, shaking, she took a sip of her coffee. No sooner was the hot liquid in her mouth than she realized her mistake. As it slid down the

AWAKENED BY THE SHEIKH

wrong way, she choked, coughed, and looked up in time to see the gaze had returned, and was fixed on her once more. Embarrassed, she tried to regain her breath.

After she'd recovered she glanced his way but he'd gone. If she'd felt uncomfortable before, she felt more so now. Not because she'd made a spectacle of herself, but because not only was the King every bit as ferocious and as forbidding as his public image, he also had an intensity that was entirely visceral and sexual. It might be just one week but it didn't look as if it was going to be an easy one.

"Is she there yet?"

Tariq narrowed his gaze at the sound of Sahmir's voice and looked around. "Who? And why are you phoning? You should be in a meeting by now."

"I'm about to go in. Before I left I arranged a little surprise for you. I just wondered if she was there."

"She? Sahmir, what have you done?" Tariq looked through the window across the courtyard to the adjoining meeting room and scanned the room. The group of three businessmen with their various hangers-on were standing together, talking confidently, their expressions smug. They believed they'd won the negotiations already. Let them, over-confidence was a weakness he could exploit. He continued to scan the room. No one out of the ordinary. Then his gaze settled on a woman, her only distinctive feature being her ability to blend into her surroundings so successfully. No, totally ordinary except… except for her eyes, which were focused on him. There was a quality in their expression that caught his attention, why he didn't know. And he didn't *need* to know. Some secretary no doubt. He continued his scan of the room before returning to the mousy assistant, now spluttering and coughing and spilling coffee onto the thickly carpeted floor. He shook his head and returned his attention to his irritating brother. "Sahmir, I don't know what you're talking about. There's no one here."

"That sexy voice? You remember? On the TV? She's your translator."

"But I don't need—" Tariq groaned as he heard the line go dead. His brother had had the audacity to put the phone down on him. He tossed away the phone and walked out of the room, towards the meeting room. He paused for a moment at the entrance and looked around once more, interested despite himself, and his gaze lingered on the mousy woman again. Her complexion and hair were pale, and her suit beige, the same color as the stone of the palace. She was like a chameleon, camouflaged by her surroundings. Curious. Inexplicably, his eyes lingered on her while she fumbled with her laptop. If she was a secretary, she was an inept one, judging by the flustered way in which she was operating her computer.

He continued to scan the room, but failed to find the woman his brother had tried to foist on him. For once, it appeared Sahmir's plans hadn't come to fruition.

He nodded to his assistants who opened the door wider for him. He swept into the board room, immediately aware of the change in atmosphere. He'd become accustomed to it over the years—this chill that descended on people as soon as they saw him. It showed in their eyes. A wariness entered them as if they didn't understand him, as if they were scared of him. It had always been that way. He'd been bewildered by it as a youth, confused as to why people wouldn't warm to him, simply based on the fact he was tall, broad, and *not* handsome. But he'd had come to appreciate its effect, especially since he'd become King. Fear was a more useful tool than affection.

He walked over to the head of the delegation and greeted

him, noting the faltering arrogance as he too responded to his presence. He knew that in some strange way his lack of beauty contributed to people's response to him. His height, solid features and immutable sense of self and purpose conveyed a sense of power which he found extremely useful. It meant he could get what he wanted in half the time his brother would have taken. He had no need to charm, to cajole, all he had to do was instruct. It might not win him friends, but he didn't need friends. He had a country to run.

He greeted the leader of the delegation in Arabic, the native language of Ma'in, and extended his hand. The man's eyes held confusion at the words he obviously didn't understand, but Tariq had no intention of translating them. If the man had the arrogance to expect a successful business meeting without even learning a few basic words of Arabic, then that was his problem. Tariq gripped the man's wavering hand. It was damp and limp and Tariq dropped it with disdain. Tariq glanced at his assistant.

"His Royal Highness, King Tariq ibn Saleh al-Fulan, welcomes you and invites you to be seated for the preliminary meeting before we proceed to his desert castle—Qusayr Zarqa— for dinner tonight, followed by a series of meetings which will conclude at the end of the week."

It was only after the sea of heads had seated that he noticed the young woman again, standing unsure, at the end of the room, as if wondering where to sit. He frowned. Why hadn't one of her party assigned her a seat? He caught the eye of his assistant and indicated the woman. He was too far away to hear what they were saying to each other. But he could see his assistant's confusion. Despite that, the woman was shown a place to his left, much to his surprise. Their gazes caught briefly, before she turned away, a fetching blush suffusing her pale skin. Tariq turned to his assistant who came up to him and whispered discreetly in his ear.

"Your translator, Your Majesty."

Tariq narrowed his eyes. "Do you have other plans, Aarif?" he asked dryly in Arabic. "You've decided to give yourself the week off?"

The assistant didn't smile but handled his papers nervously. "No, Your Majesty. It seems to be something your brother, Prince Sahmir has arranged."

His eyes shot back to the woman who was fiddling with her laptop. This young woman was the woman with the sexy voice from the advertisement? He could hardly connect the two. He smiled to himself. Sahmir had really got it wrong this time. Tariq sucked in a short breath of irritation but was careful not to betray it as he turned to the assembled company and opened the meeting in Arabic. He was going to speak English but he'd test her out first, see how good she was. No doubt Sahmir had paid far too much for this woman's time. She may as well earn it.

After he'd finished speaking, he inclined his head, indicating she should translate. Her blush rose over her pale skin as she became the center of attention. She was obviously unused to it. And then she spoke.

He looked down quickly at his papers as the impact of her voice hit him. It *was* the voice from the television. So Sahmir had been as good as his word. Despite his irritation at his brother's playfulness, he was transfixed. Her voice played over his skin like fingertips trailing along his arm, his chest and up his neck… and elsewhere. He almost expected her to reach over and place her lips on his. He licked them in readiness but didn't move, didn't alter his otherwise impassive face. But he couldn't control his reactions. He actually felt his skin prickle under the onslaught of the rich, honeyed tones, like the soothing yet stimulating brush of velvet on skin.

She had a deep, clear voice for such a small woman, textured without being husky, warm and sensuous without

AWAKENED BY THE SHEIKH

being sloppy. He could have continued to describe it, dissect it, but the one word which summed it up was sexy—she owned the most utterly sexy voice he'd ever heard. Her voice conjured up someone taller, more voluptuous, with flashing eyes that spoke of sex.

Which was the real her, he wondered? Was it her voice that was deceptive, or her appearance? He still felt the effect on his body of her words when he suddenly realized she'd stopped talking.

"We look forward to working in close collaboration with your company to further the benefits of both. I suggest we conclude your introduction shortly and my assistant will outline the agenda over the next few days."

He sat back and surrendered to the pleasure of listening to the translator's voice. He felt the blood flow to where it shouldn't. He turned and watched every man in the room. They'd all fallen under the same spell—he could see it in their eyes, in the slack fall of their mouths. Pathetic that men could be so moved by female artifice to forget what they were doing! He'd seen enough of that with his wife.

He'd often heard his mother admonish her friends for speaking ill of the dead, directly before the conversation escalated into a full scale character assassination of his father, and the full scale elevation of his mother to saint. He'd listened to it since he was a young boy sitting at her feet. It had worked. He didn't speak ill of his dead wife, but it didn't mean that he didn't know she was a money-grabbing adulterous liar. Thanks be to Allah that she'd given him children before she'd strayed. At least she'd done her duty there. He need think no more of deceitful wives. No more distractions. Especially now.

The woman began speaking again, translating one of the foreigner's fawning responses which he'd understood perfectly without the aid of a translator, not that he intended to let them know that. As she turned to Tariq, she'd drawn her chair closer and he could smell her. Not strong French perfume, but the fresh scent of her hair as it fell over her face as she inclined her head to his. He sat up straight and interrupted her. "Enough!" His voice thundered uncouthly over her honeyed tones. He rose. "Gentlemen,"—he looked at the translator and then back to the men—"we will meet within the hour at Qusayr Zarqa. It will give you the opportunity to see the desert first hand, as well as a castle thirteen centuries old which contain the rarest of Ma'in's antiquities." He walked out of the room without a backward glance, beckoning for his assistant to follow him. Once the doors were closed he spoke.

"The translator."

"Your Highness. I am sorry. We did not know she was coming until she arrived. I will pay her off, if it pleases you. As you say, there is no need—"

Tariq raised his hand and the assistant stopped abruptly. "My brother can be hasty. But…" He paused, remembering the effect of her voice on him, a feeling that he knew he wouldn't be able to forget in a hurry. He should dismiss her. He *should*. But that brief taste of her voice was like a drug. He wanted to hear it again, to experience its effect on his body. He shrugged his shoulders. "It's done. We'll live with it."

"But Your Highness, we haven't had time to do the usual security clearance, the police checks, all that is necessary for someone to work at the palace."

Tariq hesitated, but only for a moment. He was man enough to enjoy something from a distance, strong enough not to taste something he'd forbidden himself. He could smell the honey in the nectar, he could imagine it, but that would be all. Nothing would taint his life from now on, nothing would divert him from what he needed—to right the past wrongs these people had inflicted on his country—robbing it, and his family, of their wealth.

His father had been weak, had wanted to be a part of the modern world. But he was *not* his father. With Sahmir in Paris and him here, between them they could put an end to the drain of resources out of his country. His country may look wealthy, but the gloss and glitter rested on the finances of other countries. They'd become mere puppets to overseas capital. At their mercy. But for no longer.

The outcome of the meeting was inevitable so why not indulge himself for once? Allow himself the pleasure of listening to the beautiful voice that came from this unlikely woman for a few short days. Nothing longer of course. There was no room in his life for anything long term. But that voice —intriguing, hypnotic almost. It would add a certain piquancy to the next few days. And what harm could it do? He almost laughed at the thought as he looked at her slight frame, the straight hair, the unsure, downcast eyes. What harm could *she* do?

She stood, holding her laptop bag uncertainly, shifting her handbag further onto her shoulder as she looked around watching everyone else follow his assistant out to where a convoy of vehicles awaited.

He motioned to his assistant. "Tell Miss…"—he waved his hand at her—"that she will travel with me." He'd enjoy the sound of her voice during the journey to Qusayr Zarqa. Why not?

"Certainly, Your Highness."

He watched her jump as his assistant coughed politely beside her. He smiled to himself. What harm indeed?

CHAPTER 2

The limo eased away from the curb, down the pale pink street lined with mirrored buildings and date palms. People—some wearing western clothes, others in the traditional white robes of Ma'in—turned and stared as the limo passed, some bowing, recognizing the King's car, even though they couldn't see him through the black-tinted windows. The King didn't appear to notice, merely sat back and talked on the phone, as he had since she'd slipped into the back seat beside him.

Cara had never felt so ill at ease in her life. Why on earth had he requested her presence? He'd not said one word to her since she'd entered the limo and yet he'd specifically requested she travel with him. Had he got the wrong idea about her? She looked down at her conservative beige suit and smoothed out a crease before returning her gaze to the outside world. How could he get the wrong idea? If he had, he'd be the first.

And then there was the limo. This would have been reason enough for her to feel uncomfortable. It was huge. There was space enough to seat two people between her and the King. Thank the Lord! So different to the Mini she used to drive in England when she stayed with her grandmother. Just the thought of her grandmother's little yellow Mini zipping through Norfolk's narrow lanes made her feel sentimental.

She sighed and focused on the passing scenery. She just had to get through this and then she'd have enough to pay off her debts and start afresh. For all her feelings for England, she'd not be living there again—it held too many sad memories. No, she'd start afresh in Italy. But she'd miss this small, exotic country, with its modern city built along the sweeping bay of the gulf coast and its desert plains in which the old Ma'inese culture could still be found. She'd miss it, but she had no choice but to leave.

Yes, she had enough reasons to feel ill at ease but the biggest one was sitting beside her. She stole a quick glance out of the corner of her eye at the King. Her initial impression of strength and arrogance hadn't changed. He was even more impressive close up. She could only see his profile—as strong and as uncompromising as everything else about him—as he checked out the computer screen. His white robes fell in folds from broad shoulders down to long legs that stretched out in front of him. He had a stillness of movement that was unnerving. There was no change in expression, no drumming of fingers, no hesitation when he spoke. His words were brief, to the point, and his movements economical, as if uncertainty was an unknown word to him. And why wouldn't he be confident? He was the supreme ruler in this privileged and wealthy world.

She shifted her crossed arms and returned her gaze to that wealthy world. She'd seen no slums, no poverty in Ma'in. Rich as Croesus, and the richest of them all was sitting here beside her. He, and his country, were a world away from her and that's how she needed it to be. She just needed her own bag of gold and then she'd be on her way. She sighed. God, how long until they reached Qusayr Zarqa?

Suddenly the bright sunlight gave way to the white lights of a tunnel. A light was turned on inside the limo and she was confronted with her face staring back at her, pale and anxious. She looked down abruptly—she didn't need a reminder that she didn't fit into this glamorous world—her fingers immediately shifting to the place her wedding ring used to be, fingering it as if it was still there, needing the reassurance it had always given her. But it wasn't there any more. She took a deep breath and looked back into the window that reflected the limo's interior, straight into the King's gaze. She turned away but it was too late. She'd reminded him she was there. He put down the phone with a curt response and turned to her. She felt physically compelled to meet that intense gaze.

"So, Miss…" He narrowed his eyes. "I don't believe we've been formally introduced. I apologize for the omission."

Cara was struck by his courtesy, so at odds with his awesome impression. She was also struck by his perfect English. This wasn't someone who needed a translator. Not for English anyway. "Oh," she said, feeling flustered. "Carin —" she stopped herself just in time. Giving the full name she was given at birth wasn't a clever idea. "Cara Devlin."

He inclined his head regally and extended his hand to hers. "A pleasure to meet you, Miss Devlin." She held out her hand and he gripped it in a warm clinch. She'd expected something crushing, like his persona, but it wasn't. It was firm, warm, engulfing, but somehow she knew he'd restrained his strength in that grip, aware of her much smaller boned hand in his. She looked up and couldn't help smiling at this unexpected sensitivity. But there was no smile given in return. He might be polite but he obviously didn't do smiling. She felt her own smile waver. Her husband had always said she was an open book, that whatever she thought or felt was instantly registered on her face.

His eyes swept over her in one long, lingering glance before settling on her eyes. He nodded, once, as if coming to some decision. He sat back, facing her. "Talk to me."

She frowned, confused. Of all the things she expected, an invitation to talk about anything was bottom of the list. Had she missed something? "I'm sorry, um"—she shook her head—"what would you like me to talk about?"

"Anything. Tell me about yourself, if you wish."

"What would you like to know?"

"Anything you wish to share with me. It was my brother who hired you, I know little about you and you appear to have successfully evaded our security checks."

Cara blanched. It was just as well, or else she might not have got the job. "Well, of course I can complete the paperwork if you need me to." She kept her crossed fingers out of sight. He wouldn't want her if he knew who she was married to.

He dismissed her suggestion with a careless wave of the arm. "I don't think that's required. I doubt you're a threat to national security."

Sometimes, Cara thought, it was useful to appear insignificant.

"You work as an interpreter, I understand?" he continued.

"Yes. Interpreter, translator." Did he really not know why Prince Sahmir had hired her? "And… I do some voice-over work for an advertising agency."

"Ah, yes. Chocolate, wasn't it?"

She bit her lip, embarrassed at the memory of her suggestive lines. "And cars," she continued hastily, "and a hotel chain."

"Anything that requires an alluring voice." His eyes

narrowed, but through what emotion, she couldn't say. His face was otherwise as inscrutable as ever. "A *persuasive* voice."

"Well, um, I guess."

"And your language skills. Tell me of these. I'm told you're fluent in Portuguese and Japanese, and understand my own language well."

"Yes."

Suddenly the pressure in the car changed and they emerged from the tunnel. Cara turned and blinked out at the bright sunshine before turning back to him. He'd sat back in his seat, observing her as if for the first time, rubbing his finger against his lips thoughtfully.

"Unusual," he murmured.

She frowned. "My languages?"

He blinked as if trying to regain a train of thought. "Of course. For an English woman, such skill with languages is not common."

"Maybe. But my mother was from Brazil and I majored in Japanese at university." She shrugged. "The Arabic, I've just picked up."

"You are clever. That's good. It could prove useful if you listen to everything that's being said, both in and outside the meetings and report back to me."

She frowned. "Spy on your guests, you mean?"

He raised an eyebrow in query. "Guests? Yes I suppose they are. But not for pleasure. For business only. And as for spying. Did I use the word?"

"Well, no, but—"

"Then I doubt that is what I meant. You are in my employ and I wish you to interpret what you hear and report it back to me. I trust you are happy with that?" His tone was ice-cold. A shiver snaked down her back. He was the King and he was telling her to remember that.

"Yes, of course, Your Royal Highness."

He nodded and was silent for a moment, his eyes still fixed on her, assessing her. "And has my assistant advised you about the subject of the meeting?"

She shook her head. "No."

"Then I shall. You will need to know the context in order to be effective. Thirty years ago, Miss Devlin, my father invited investors into our country. They arrived to see a land that appeared empty to them." He turned back and glanced out of the window at the empty desert which now spread out on both sides of them. "And, indeed it appeared empty to my father, whose vision was filled with the cities he'd seen at university, in America and Europe. He wanted to be King of a land full of the glories of the civilization for which he so yearned."

He fell silent and Cara followed his gaze out to the apparent monotony of the desert. "Not a land of desert."

He turned to her and searched her eyes for a few moments. "No, not a land of desert. A city. A city of towers, of wealth, of motor cars, machinery, finance. A mirage of light and magic. And he succeeded. Those visitors gave my father everything he could have wished for."

He fell silent again and Cara felt some sort of comment was required. "Well, that was a good outcome then."

"No, Miss Devlin, it wasn't. However that thirty-year contract has now expired and we are here to renew the terms."

Cara blinked nervously. She hadn't realized the meeting was so important.

"And that is why, Miss Devlin, I would be grateful for your cooperation in this matter. I want you everywhere these men are. I want you to listen to what they have to say and I want you to report back everything you hear to me."

She nodded, but frowned. "And you trust me to do this? I

mean, I *am* trustworthy, but you don't know that. As you say, I've had no checks done."

"I trust no one. Not you, not the people I do business with, nor my staff. No one. But I trust my own instincts and I can tell a lie from a truth. Tell me the truth and we will get along just fine." He sat back in his seat, scrutinizing her intently. He nodded briefly. "You are quick to blush, Miss Devlin." She blushed instantly. He smiled. "I somehow doubt you are a security risk. I doubt very much you'd ever get away with a lie. Now, we have a little time before we arrive, talk to me."

That same instruction again. What the hell was she going to talk about? He must have noted her confusion.

"Anything," he continued. "Tell me how long you have been in my country."

Cara swallowed. She hadn't expected an interrogation. She shrugged, hoping to appear casual. "A couple of years."

"And you came here, why?"

She hesitated only for a moment as the image of her husband, Piers, flitted through her mind, urging her to leave her corporate job in London and travel with him to Ma'in where his contacts told him his import-export business would flourish. It hadn't been such a big decision. After all, she'd been there before, with her father.

She looked up, caught King Tariq's eyes and flashed a quick smile, hoping it would dissolve the hated memory. "I came here with a friend, and just stayed." Lies, she knew, would not go undetected, but she might get away with being economical with the truth.

"And you like my country?"

She smiled. "It's fabulous."

He frowned. "The city, you mean?"

She shrugged. "Well, yes, but I've also traveled into the desert and visited the Old Cities. They're amazing."

"So you appreciate my country's past." He nodded approvingly. "Then you will be interested in our destination. It was the home of my ancestors. It was originally one of the Desert Castles that ran along the spice route from the East, through to the Mediterranean. While our roots lie with the Bedouin, our position here, at a strategic point on the seas, means our history is greatly influenced by Persia. Hence a blend of cultures, a rich cultural heritage, the remnants which can be seen all around." He followed her gaze. "If you know where to look." He pursed his lips. "Unfortunately, too rich for some to withstand temptation." He turned to her once more, as if remembering her presence. "So, do you intend to stay in Ma'in?"

She shook her head, biting her lip as she immediately regretted the negation.

King Tariq raised his eyebrow in query. "Why not, if you like it so much? My vision of Ma'in may not be in accord with my father's, but I welcome people who can contribute to my country's economy."

She looked down at her clasped hands, wondering how she could get out of this interrogation, wondering why on earth a King would ask her such questions. "I want to start a new life in Italy.

"Italy is your home?"

A very good question. She shrugged. "No. I don't really have one. The nearest thing I have to it is England—a small village in Norfolk. The place I used to visit my grandmother. But I won't go back there. There's nothing for me there, nothing but rain and clouds." She couldn't help shivering.

"Tell me about it."

She frowned. When was the interrogation going to stop? Surely he couldn't really be interested in her? "It's pretty, a very old village. In summer it has many visitors, retracing the route of medieval pilgrims." She paused and looked up at him, hoping he was bored. But his expression was still inscrutable, unchanged.

"Go on," he said.

"My grandmother died last year. Her house has been sold but she left me a shop in the centre of the old village, above which is a small apartment. It looks out to the medieval well in the market place. Beyond that are the gates to the Abbey." She took a deep breath. "It's surrounded by fields of wheat, the brilliant yellow of rape seed, ancient medieval churches. It's very beautiful, quiet. But I've only visited there." She glanced down at her hands clasped anxiously in her lap, her fingers seeking out the empty place on her ring finger. She tore her hands apart and looked out at the arid landscape they were now in.

She'd said too much. She wasn't used to anyone wanting to know anything about her. She was always the listener, not the talker. But once she started to describe the only place that had ever felt like home, the words had tumbled out.

"Surely your family and friends would be pleased to see you return to Norfolk?"

He may not be smiling but his eyes had grown warmer, as if he was interested. Something melted inside her then. *He was truly interested*. It was an odd feeling. She smiled. "I have no family any more. I'm an only child and my parents are both dead. And well, I don't know many people there either. No, I don't intend to return to England for good. I can make my home anywhere."

She waited. There were no murmurs of sympathy, no awkward looks. Just a matter of fact acceptance of her words.

"So your home is just a place…interesting. I consider many places in the world beautiful, but this"—he gestured ahead of them, to a building that was slowly emerging out of the rocky terrain—"is my home."

She followed his gaze to the sprawling, ancient adobe building that she'd thought at first to be a part of the hills that fringed the stony plain. But as they grew closer its square uncompromising facade was revealed. At each corner rounded turrets protruded. Its front entrance was framed with a three story high arch and along the top, the facade was pierced with square windows. "Home? It looks… well, it looks very different to your city palace."

For the first time she caught a glimmer of a smile. "It is." He inclined a little toward her and she smelled his aftershave, as masculine as he was, and felt his warm breath on her cheek. "And *that*, Miss Devlin, is why I call it home."

She looked up at him, startled by the confidence. He was close, so close she could see the subtle colors in his eyes, which from a distance looked black, but close up, contained shades of chestnut brown, and a dark gold. It must have been for a moment only that he lingered, so close to her, not touching, not being disrespectful, but it was enough to send a flare of heat through her body. She could feel it lighting up her face but she couldn't move away. She was mesmerized by those eyes that remained fixed on hers. She swallowed. "It suits you." It was only when she saw her words register on his face and the first smile rest briefly on his lips that she realized how personal her comment was. She sat back hurriedly. "I'm sorry, I just mean…" She trailed off, flustered.

But he didn't move, simply allowed his gaze to range briefly over her face. "I know what you mean, and you are quite correct. The city palace was a product of my father's aspirations. The desert palace we are going to, was the place I was raised by my grandfather, the place where my family lived for many generations before the city was even thought of. It is where I belong." He tilted his head to one side. "We all have to belong somewhere, do we not, Miss Devlin?"

She shrugged, unable to agree. Besides, what was the

point of belonging when all the people you loved had left you? His smile slipped away as the limo pulled up in front of the entrance, the other cars following behind. Their doors were suddenly opened but the King didn't leave immediately.

"I hope you enjoy your stay, Miss Devlin." He paused as he held her gaze.

She nodded, speechless, as she wondered how she'd managed to slip into such a personal, deep conversation with His Royal Highness, Tariq ibn Saleh al-Fulan, King of Ma'in and supreme sheikh of his people? It was as if he really wanted to know all about her, the *real* her. And how disarming, how unusual was that? He really seemed to want to hear what she had to say. She smiled. "I think I will."

He got out of the limo and then turned and ducked his head to speak once more to her. "You have a very beautiful voice. I look forward to hearing more of it."

Biting disappointment burned away her pleasure as she watched him walk up to the palace entrance, people falling into step behind him. The intimate spell, broken by the compliment. It was her voice. That's all. Just her voice he wanted to hear, nothing that she'd said. All he'd wanted was to hear her talk. He hadn't wanted to learn more about her, or her world. Of course he hadn't. Why would he have done? Yet again, she'd been sucked into believing someone was interested in her, for herself alone. And yet again she'd been wrong.

Still, at least she understood now, before it went too far. She smoothed her hair down with shaking hands before stepping out of the car, which an assistant had returned to open for her. A wall of heat hit her after the air conditioning in the car. It pressed against her skin, her lungs, searing her throat as she tried to breathe. Quickly she followed the others inside the fortress-like building, filled as much with blistering disappointment as with the heat of the desert air.

The group of men from Aurus walked around the reception hall, craning their necks to look up at the ancient Islamic architecture and the wall paintings depicting hunting scenes, animals and birds.

"Amazing! What a pile!"

Tariq pretended not to understand. "The castle was built around the eighth century," he said in Arabic, "as a fortress and a pleasure palace for my forefathers. That wall painting"—he pointed to an image which, although ancient, was still fresh in color and detail—"shows the Caliph, the haloed figure, surrounded by kings he vanquished including the Byzantine emperor and the Visigothic King of Spain." Tariq pointed to the far side of the hall. "And over there is the hammam—the bath complex." He gestured for them to follow him as Cara translated.

He strode into the centre of the hammam and waited for the gasps of admiration to die down, as the men craned their necks to look up at the zodiac fresco, high up on the domed ceiling of the caldarium. "This is the hot room, and as you can see, my people appreciated fine art."

"That's not all," shouted one of the group, laughing after Cara's translation. "Looks like they knew how to enjoy themselves too, if those images are anything to go by."

Tariq ignored their comments—they were crass and to be expected. It irritated him to suffer their presence in his home. But what was more fitting venue than this castle—a symbol of his country and his culture—in which to claim back his inheritance? He glanced around at the uplifted faces of the businessmen. "Welcome to Qusayr Zarqa, gentleman. Please settle in and make yourself comfortable. I'll leave you with Aarif and will join you again for dinner, in a few hours' time. I wish you a pleasant stay."

Cara duly translated while the men ignored her, as they gazed, fascinated, at the soaring vaulted ceilings and frescoes. Tariq watched her as she did the same, and wondered. Wondered how on earth he'd not noticed her eyes before. As they'd sat together in the limousine, when her eyes had only been illuminated by the fluorescent glow of the electric lights that lined the tunnel, the whites of her eyes had caught his gaze as he'd seen her watching him. Clear and steady, they'd called to him like a beacon of salvation. And he'd answered, concluding his phone call.

And then, as they'd emerged once more into the full light of day, color had sparked into her irises. Green. She had green eyes. At first he'd have called them hazel. Not that the thought had occurred to him to call them anything. Only now. Now that he'd seen that they were an amalgam of many colors, but predominantly green, the green of sweet relief. How had he missed that?

CHAPTER 3

*N*ight had fallen outside the open windows of the dining hall and made its presence felt, despite the brilliance of the chandeliers overhead. The electric lights formed mere pools of light in the cavernous room, between which the opaque darkness claimed its territory.

Tariq looked around the room, silent and watchful. He always preferred to observe; he'd found you could learn so much more that way. He'd learned the hard way that people's smiles, their superficial talk, were like the deceptive sweep of wind-smoothed sand—dangerous if you didn't know where to place your feet. It was second nature to him, now, to understand what went on beneath the surface.

He knew what these men were thinking, what they wanted. The company they represented had had their own way for the past generation. For thirty years he'd suffered their invasive presence. They thought it was going to continue, but it wasn't. They just hadn't realized it yet.

One of the Aurus executives, Mahito, turned to him and spoke in English, his fascination with the castle apparently made him more interested in being understood. "It's impressive, this place."

"Thank you," replied Tariq guardedly, also in English.

"But, you know, a week here? We can get this contract signed here, now, tonight."

"That is not the Ma'inese way."

"Come on, what's the hold up? Why the delay? You've a contractual right to buy us out. You haven't done so. What's the point in waiting? Sign for another thirty years and we'll be on our way."

"But, if we don't buy you out, you also have a right to transfer your holdings to a different site. Surely you'd like to investigate your options before signing?"

Mahito shrugged. "It's all the same to us. I haven't heard there's any better seam of gold than the one we're already working." Then Mahito's eyes suddenly narrowed with interest. "Is there?"

It was Tariq's turn to shrug. Tariq had to stall. Sahmir hadn't come up with the funds yet. With the seed of doubt sown, Tariq turned to watch Cara, who stood hesitantly on the threshold. Mahito followed Tariq's glance and then turned away, drawn into conversation by another in his party. Tariq exhaled a tightly held breath, suddenly realizing that he'd been subconsciously waiting for her.

The hum of conversation receded as he focused all his attention on her, as she walked silently over the antique rugs, their colors dimmed away from the light of the chandeliers. The different shades of the dark abaya she wore shifted—one minute midnight blue, the next, obsidian black—changing as she moved past the darting lights of the over-sized candles Tariq preferred. It was warm in the dining room, but it wasn't the desert heat rolling in through the open doors which fired his veins. He nodded to his assistant, Aarif, who rose and greeted her, and brought her over to Tariq, as instructed.

Tariq, too, stood and greeted her while she took her place beside him. She sat down and Aarif helped push her chair in behind her. Tariq sat back in the grandly carved ormolu chair and steepled his fingers, pressing them against his lips for a moment as he watched her settle. Her movements were delicate, subtle, barely noticeable. It was as if she spent her time trying *not* to be noticed. And no doubt she usually succeeded. Most of the time, except not with him. He'd suffered years of living with a very noticeable wife. Now, the opposite attracted him. If his wife, Laiha, had been like a ruby, flashing and showy, Cara was like a pearl—hidden and rare.

"So, Miss Devlin," he said in Arabic, "what do you think of Qusayr Zarqa, now you've had the leisure to inspect it?"

"It's… very grand. Very… intimidating."

"Um…" He paused as he enjoyed the sensations her voice, speaking his native tongue, created. "Yes, sometimes it's useful to appear intimidating. Especially to one's enemies."

"And do you often invite your enemies to your home?"

He smiled as he brought the glass of water to his lips. He swallowed and carefully returned the cut glass crystal goblet to the table. "Sometimes it's necessary."

"And your friends?" she asked innocently. "When you invite your friends here, aren't they intimidated?"

He was silent and for the first time since she'd sat down beside him he felt his smile slip from his lips. Within minutes she'd cut to the heart of him. He had employees, he had subjects, he had family, but he had few real friends. He'd spent his life avoiding intimacy, only focusing on what he needed to do in order to regain control of his country's wealth. He cleared his throat.

"The palace is essentially a hunting lodge—a retreat.

When my wife was alive we entertained here, to show visitors a little of our desert culture."

She raised an eyebrow and he followed her quick gaze around the opulent French revival decorations.

"You are wondering what connection the decoration and this furniture have to my culture?"

She looked uncomfortable but to her credit, held his gaze as she shrugged. "I mean no insult, Your Royal Highness. It's just that—"

"The Bedouin aren't known for their Louis XV sideboards?" He smiled and was rewarded with an embarrassed smile as she nodded. "Miss Devlin, shopping for French antiques was something of a hobby of my wife's and, besides, if we entertained the traditional way, we'd now be seated on a camel-hair blanket in a drafty tent, drinking camel's milk. It is not necessarily what our visitors would enjoy."

Her face was suddenly lit from within and a short, infectious laugh bubbled out from nowhere. He sat back in his chair as if a forceful hand had pushed him.

"No, I should imagine not and I'm sure your guests are most grateful for your consideration." The smile turned into a wry grin as she scanned the room. She indicated Mahito, who was holding his champagne glass up to the light, inspecting the color of the wine. "I overheard him mention an African safari where they 'camped' under the stars. It turned out the camp was a luxury lodge."

She turned to him and while the laughter had disappeared, her green eyes sparkled with a light he'd not seen before. It was so different, so sudden, he found it shocking… and enthralling. He should be talking to his other guests, but he didn't. He wanted to know more about this woman, who kept herself so well hidden from view.

"And you, Miss Devlin, what is your experience with camping?"

The light in her eyes suddenly changed, became misty and far-away. She took a sip of her water and looked up, but the relaxed laughter had disappeared. She was guarded, now, as if she were keeping something in check. "A drafty tent for sure. But we had sleeping bags. And milk from the farm where we camped."

"Not unlike here. Except I imagine you had less sand and more green fields."

She nodded. "That's about it. Plus a lot more rain." The grin flashed again before she took a sip of her water. But it wasn't the same.

"And you enjoyed it?"

She looked surprised at his questioning. So was he. For some reason she intrigued him. She held herself in check, hid herself, kept secrets, secrets he wanted to know.

"Yes. Very much. I'd stay with my grandmother while my parents traveled the world to different universities, and would camp in one of her fields with the neighbor's daughter. She was, and is, a good friend."

"Your parents were academics?"

"My father was."

"What was his field?"

She pressed her lips together briefly. "Antiquities."

Tariq frowned. "Antiquities? There was a Sir Thomas Devlin who visited our university in Ma'in from time to time."

She nodded. "My father."

Was it his imagination or did she suddenly look uncomfortable? "His knowledge of our ancient texts was second to none."

"Yes. He loved his subject and he loved Ma'in in particular."

"And do you share his interest?"

She shrugged and nodded evasively.

Tariq pointed to some text beneath a fresco. "Can you read that?"

She frowned at the ancient words for a few moments and then translated them perfectly.

"I'm impressed." He was more than impressed. Her skill could prove extremely useful.

"Don't be. My father was most critical of my efforts."

"Tell me about him."

"He was a great scholar but"—she flashed him an uncomfortable smile—"he hated camping. And you, Your Majesty. Have you often camped under a camel-hair blanket with only camel's milk to drink?" Not a very subtle change of subject. Despite that, he melted a little at the smile that flickered on her lips with a disarming cheekiness.

He smiled. "Please, call me Tariq. If you are going to ask me such impertinent questions, we should be on first name terms."

She hesitated briefly before nodding. "And, please, call me Cara."

"So, Cara, in answer to your question, yes, I spent much time as a small boy with my grandparents in the desert. I preferred to be there, rather than in the city which was a building site when my father was creating the city you see today."

"Was there much to keep a young boy entertained in the desert?"

"Oh yes! I spent my time with the animals, riding, hunting."

"What did you hunt?"

"Gazelles, hares and ibex. With salukis. The Bedouin way is to throw the dogs from horseback so they have a head start…"

"Wow!" She blinked. "I've never heard of that before. It sounds… bloodthirsty and thrilling, both at the same time."

"It was. But no more so than the English, hunting with dogs. At least with us, the end is quicker. And we do not look as ridiculous hunting as you English with your uniforms, tradition and quaint expressions."

He was rewarded with another brief laugh. "Do you still hunt?"

"When I can. It gives me a chance to be with my tribe, my grandfather's people."

"You weren't raised by your parents?"

"My father took over as King when he was young and lived in the city with my mother, sister, and two younger brothers. I did not see eye to eye with my father. Everything I know of value today, I learned from my grandfather." He stopped speaking, aware he was telling this stranger things only his family knew. Like so many sensitive, empathetic people she had an ability to draw confidences from people. He suddenly realized they'd both shifted in their seats so they were facing each other, their heads dipped close to each other's, as if to shut out the noise in the hall. He twisted away from her. "And you, too, lived away from your parents periodically?"

"Only when they traveled either for my father's work, or my mother's. My mother was a musician who traveled a lot with work until, well, my father got sick and…"

She blinked and looked down at her fingers which fidgeted in her lap. He suddenly realized that, for the first time in many years, he was completely absorbed in someone else—her thoughts, her past, her feelings, her sheer physicality. As she rubbed one hand against the other, he could have almost sworn he could feel the firm rub of her fingers against his hand. The way her narrow fingers tapered to a plain, unpolished nail, captivated him, held his full attention, as if it were the answer to a question he'd asked.

"Your Highness." Aarif, his assistant, broke the spell. "Mr Hironaka—"

"Please call me Mahito. We are all friends here."

Aarif bowed his head and continued. "Mahito was just saying that he's heard about the collection of priceless early Islamic art kept here."

Of course he had. Tariq had made sure the men had heard. Tariq nodded to Aarif. He could always depend on his assistant to keep him on track. Not that he usually needed it. But the soft rustling of Cara's abaya, as she shifted in her seat, threatened his usual focus. "Indeed. It would be my pleasure to show you after dinner tonight, if you wish."

Satisfied that things were going according to plan, Tariq allowed his attention to stray back to the woman at his side. He leaned a little closer to her, to inhale her fresh, subtle perfume. She smelled as if she'd brushed passed the orange blossom that flowered in the central courtyard and it somehow still clung to her. Irrationally he felt that, if he lifted her pale, silky hair, the fragrance would be intensified behind her ear.

"That would be great," said Mahito, stubbornly insisting on speaking in Japanese. Tariq had known that Mahito was the driving force of the Aurus contingent, but hadn't realized just how powerful he was until he'd seen their interactions. The man was barely into middle age, had been handsome once, but easy living had made his features flaccid, his eyes rheumy. Tariq felt a flare of disgust at the man's lack of strength. These men had too much of everything, and valued nothing. "Worth a fortune on the open market, I would think," Mahito continued, speaking loudly as if believing Tariq was somehow hearing impaired. "That's not of interest to you Ma'inese, of course."

Cara hesitated a moment, looking embarrassed at the man's ignorance, but when she began translating, Tariq forgot everything. She omitted the insulting nuances and gave the translation an elegance and deference entirely missing from the original.

Tariq replied noncommittally, watching the light of the candles flicker on Cara's soft cheeks. Somehow the pallor he'd noticed earlier didn't have the effect of making her look insignificant, now. It looked subtle beside the other man's florid cheeks; it looked as if it would feel like silk beneath a fingertip.

Tariq nodded to Aarif who engaged Mahito in conversation. As soon as he'd turned away, Tariq bowed his head close to Cara. "Your translation was inaccurate."

Cara looked startled. "I'm sorry, I just thought—"

"Thought you would add a little courtesy to the man's conversation." He nodded, approvingly. "That was very considerate of you."

"I didn't realize you knew Japanese," Cara said.

"I know many languages, but I find it more… convenient for this not to be known. It can be very revealing." He sat back slowly.

"And what, exactly are you hoping will be revealed?"

"The truth."

She glanced away briefly, a light blush resting on those pale cheeks. "And that's so easily revealed if people are ignorant of your knowledge of their language?"

"Indeed. It leads to an arrogance on their part and a slipping of their guard." He took the advantage of moving his head to hers as if imparting a confidence. "It's always good to know your enemy, Cara. And if, in the process you get them to underestimate you, relax and reveal their true thoughts, so much the better."

She looked up at him suddenly, those green eyes as dark as a shadowed pool, and he forgot everything—not just what he was thinking, but where he was, even *who* he was.

"Your enemy? I wasn't aware this was a battle, Your Highness."

He inhaled a long slow breath as he suddenly realized he'd let his own guard down with her, and told her how he really saw these businessmen. They *were* his enemy. But only he should be aware of that.

"Only in so far as any business negotiation is a battle, Miss Devlin. Have you heard of *The Art of War*? That book is much used in business practices. It is merely one way of looking at a negotiation."

Aarif's attempt at diverting Mahito had stalled and, much to Tariq's irritation, Mahito turned once more to Tariq. "Those antiquities you mention. I heard some of them were stolen last year."

Tariq flexed his fingers before curling them into fists, out of sight of his guests. Mahito turned to Cara, waiting for her to translate.

Tariq closed his eyes briefly as her voice curled around his gut like fingers and pulled, his blood racing to the place that wanted her. Silence followed.

"We retrieved most of it."

"Did you catch the thief?"

Cara's beautiful voice faltered a little in the translation and Tariq glanced at her sharply.

"No. We had no concrete proof but the chief suspect is in prison in France, for another crime."

The sudden swing of Cara's bright hair as she moved her chair away from the table caught his eye. Tariq turned to her, frowning. "You're not leaving yet?" He realized his tone had the imperiousness of a statement when she sat down again.

"I'm… I'm feeling a little tired."

"Surely you don't wish to miss seeing the treasures Qusayr Zarqa holds? With your father so knowledgeable about them, I'd have thought you'd be curious."

She nodded hesitantly. "Yes, of course."

"Then we will go now." He rose. "Gentlemen, if you'd follow me."

It was past midnight by the time they reached the antiquities room, down ancient stairs and into a cool, stone-lined basement, far below the ground level, lit by discreet lighting. Tariq punched a code into the panel.

"State-of-the-art security? I'd have thought it was safe out here, in the middle of nowhere," Mahito commented in English.

Tariq ground his teeth as he tried not to rise to the bait. "A desert doesn't stop thieves. I'd have thought you'd have known that."

He could tell from the other man's expression that he had no idea that Tariq was referring to him and his colleagues.

"Oh, yes. That burglary you mentioned earlier, it was from this palace?"

"No. It was in the city. Everything has since been moved to here."

He turned to Cara who stood behind him. He knew she was there, he could sense it. "Miss Devlin"—he reverted to the formal, he had no desire to hear these foreigners refer to her by her first name—"you might be interested in these maps."

"Why would she be?" asked one of the men.

"Because Miss Devlin's father was a Professor at Cambridge University and a fine scholar of ancient Arabic texts."

The man's eyebrow shot up. "Sir Thomas Devlin was *your* father?"

"Yes."

"So that's why your Arabic is so good."

"It may be good," said Tariq. "But this script is archaic. Beyond even Miss Devlin's skills, I think."

Cara peered at the map, focusing on the intricate text, its spider thin loops and whorls, half-obscured by age. She tilted her head to one side, concentrating now. "No." She looked up at Tariq with an expression of intense interest. She was in her element, he could see. "I can read it easily. It describes the place on the map"—she glanced up at the illuminated heading—"Jabal al Kanz, as being 'a land of treasure, hidden and valuable, a place where the old religions were worshiped, a life-enriching place to be treasured for ever.'"

Tariq glanced around the men discreetly. As he'd anticipated Cara's words held the men's rapt attention. They were spellbound by the archaic description of the word 'treasure', just as he thought they would be. In their greed the men had forgotten their disdain for Cara, who was now the center of attention.

"Treasure? What kind of treasure? Does it say?"

Tariq watched Cara's face intently. How much would she know? A frown settled between her brows as if she was trying to puzzle something out. "Gold, I think. But—"

"Gold!" Any further elaboration was lost by the excited talk that broke out among the men. "Gold, Your Royal Highness? You didn't mention you had other seams of gold on your land. Why aren't you mining them?"

"You heard Miss Devlin. The place is sacred to our people."

"Like the first gold mine was to your father?"

Tariq winced inwardly at the rudeness. "Gentlemen, it's late. I suggest we retire now." He walked to the door and waited as his assistant held it open.

"But… the map is intriguing. Can we learn more?"

"Maybe later."

The men muttered and left the room reluctantly, chivvied

on by Aarif. Soon the last had left. Tariq closed the door softly. Cara was still poring over the old map, concentrating hard. He walked up behind her and allowed himself the luxury of simply observing her for a few moments. There was something so pure about her. She loved the map for what it was—something rare and beautiful—not for what it could give her.

"The others have left, Cara."

She looked around abstractedly. "Oh, I didn't hear them."

"No, you were too absorbed in the map."

Her fingers were splayed over the glass cabinet as if she were touching the fragile parchment. "It's beautiful," she breathed.

He dipped his head towards hers as if to examine the map. In reality he wanted to be closer to her.

"Look, here." She pointed to one particular piece of text. "It uses that word 'treasure' again, except this time in a different context—as 'life-giving.'"

"Come." He reached down and took her hand and pulled her away from the cabinet. Her attitude changed immediately.

"Tariq… Your Highness, I mean."

"Tariq is fine. There is no need to look so wary, it is simply time to leave here. That's all."

She nodded, hesitantly, as if not understanding. But then, neither did he. He still held her hand and the feel of her skin against his nearly drove all rational thought from his mind. Nearly. He needed to get her away from the map. *Now*. He didn't want her to understand its real meaning. *That* would be of no interest to the Aurus Group; *that* wouldn't divert them for long enough.

Reluctantly he let go her hand and stepped away, indicating she should precede him to the door. With her head bowed she did so. He watched her, not moving himself.

"You should lift your head, Cara."

She looked up at him and he still saw the mists of confusion she was trying to hide. "Why?"

"Because people don't see you for who you really are."

"Maybe that's a good thing." Her voice was almost a whisper. It took all his effort to restrain himself from moving closer to her.

"It's never a good thing. Look up. Look as high as you can and claim the space around you."

He stepped forward and tilted her chin up, and his breath caught in his throat. A beam of bright light from a display above the door caught the line of her jaw, highlighting her creamy skin. He fought the urge to stroke the line with his fingers that still rested under her chin, to trace it, to touch that softness that was so elusive to him in the harsh light of the day. But then he saw a look of recognition enter her eyes, swiftly followed by horror and confusion. He turned away frowning, uncomfortable to have seen someone's feelings so direct and unhidden, and looked up to see what had inspired such a reaction. It was only a small ancient statue in a recessed area above the door. He looked back at her.

"It was once one of a pair. The other has disappeared."

"Stolen…"

Her face was suddenly paler, if that were possible. Perhaps it was the light that shone on her from directly overhead? He frowned and turned back to the statue. "Indeed. Last year. The one last treasure, still missing.

"But…but, you said it had all been recovered. It hasn't been in the news."

"We recovered all but one of the artifacts. And no, it's not been publicized. I didn't wish it to be known. I don't want the world believing people can rob my country of its treasures and get away with it. Also, that way, the piece will be unable to be validated, so the thief will be unable to sell it for what it's worth."

"How much is it worth?" Her voice was barely a whisper.

"Given the lack of them on the open market, it's priceless. But it's not about money. To me, to my countrymen, it's our culture that's been pillaged." He shook his head in despair. "People want to try to take such things from our country, but we have ways of dealing with them. Such people try to reach in and grab the heart of one. That is the worst thing—to take someone's identity. We are not lenient in such cases."

He was suddenly aware of total quiet. The hum of the air conditioning was the only sound. No noise from outside could enter the insulated walls. He turned to the woman beside him. She looked away and took a few steps back. She put a hand to her forehead and brushed back her hair. To his surprise a gleam of sweat glistened there.

"Are you feeling unwell?"

"I'm fine. But…I think I should go to bed."

"Of course. Perhaps the air conditioning after the heat of the desert has affected you. Besides, it's late."

He turned, punched in a code into the keypad and opened the door for her. She kept her head down as she had before, not meeting his eyes as she walked by. It was only when she passed him that the breeze from the corridor lifted her hair aside and he caught a glimpse once more of the definite line of her jaw, creating a contrast to the softness of her cheeks and full lips. He felt a thrill ripple through his body and settle inside him. He closed the door, reset the alarm and joined her. They ascended the steps in silence. Once in the hall he pointed to the far staircase.

"Your room is that way. I wish you goodnight." He walked away before she could turn to him, before he could see her eyes, before she could say anything that might make him take her hand in his and pull her to his bedroom. As he walked through the echoing corridor, so empty, so beautiful, he wondered why he hadn't taken her hand. He'd taken women here before. But he knew. It was because this wasn't a simple sexual transaction. She stirred him like the shamal wind of the dawn star—the Barih Thorayya—lifting the sand and whirling it around before settling it into new, unknown patterns.

The sound of her, the look of her, the accidental touch of her, didn't stop on his surface, didn't stay as a stimulus in his brain to be understood, but drove down deeper, beyond the superficial, to a place he really didn't want to go. Because he didn't know what lay there, buried after so many years of bitterness.

Cara walked blindly down the beautiful corridor towards her room. The image of the lone statue was ingrained in her mind. She'd seen it so briefly yet she knew every curve, every nuance of the beautiful object. She knew the flow and form of it, the texture of the stone, the expression in the woman's eye. She knew because it because she'd lived with its pair for a year, in total ignorance of where it had come from, or of how valuable it was.

Before he'd left, her husband had cleverly convinced her it was one of the replicas he'd originally traded in. The very fact he'd left it with her had confirmed it. But now she realized that he'd have returned for it, if he hadn't had to flee the country. As it was, he'd run from one set of charges, straight into another and he'd been convicted in France for an earlier theft. His criminal past had finally caught up with him. His import/export business had turned out to be less about import and more about smuggling treasures out of the country.

She'd helped the Ma'inese Police as much as she could but

she knew little and had been cleared of any wrongdoing. But all the while, the statue had been sitting, half-hidden, on her book shelf.

And here she was with the man from whom her husband had stolen it. Her immediate impulse had been to tell the King where he could find the treasure. She'd only just stopped herself in time. Her innocence might no longer be believed. She might be thrown into jail. As the King said, and as she knew from Islamic justice, the penalty would be harsh. At best, her bank account would be frozen and she'd be deported—penniless and alone. No, she couldn't risk it. She'd make sure the statue was returned, but only once she'd left the country.

In the meantime, she had to face the King, every day for the next week. If he knew of her connection, God knows what he would do to her. She couldn't risk lifting her eyes to his and telling him everything that was in her soul. Whatever the nascent feelings that stirred in her when she was with him, she had to ignore them, ignore the flash of desire in his eyes that was so seductive.

Because to do anything else would be to throw herself at the mercy of Tariq. And mercy wasn't a word she connected with the King—revenge was, anger was, but not generosity towards his enemies.

As she opened the door to her room, her mind went back to the statue, still sitting on her bookshelf in her apartment. It was in the wrong place. Just like her.

CHAPTER 4

Cara paced the stone-flagged floor of her bedroom back and forth as she tried to figure out how on earth she was going to face Tariq. Every time she thought about the statue, sitting squashed between random books on her bookshelf, she blushed guiltily. She'd never been able to hide her thoughts or feelings. Maybe that was why Piers, her husband, had hidden so much from her.

She stopped pacing and looked out the open window. The fragrance of lemon and lime flowers rose from the oasis gardens below and the muezzin's call to prayer filled the air, soothing and stirring her at the same time, just as her mother's music had so many years ago. No, she thought, Piers never told her anything because he knew she'd have run a mile if she'd known what he was up to.

She wondered if she'd ever really loved him. To begin with she'd been grateful for his attentions and kindness, definitely, seduced by his love-making, perhaps a little. But all the while he'd been using her, and her father's knowledge about the Ma'inese artifacts. And once she'd outlived her usefulness, he'd gone.

But the nightmare was nearly over now. She just had to get through this week and then, as soon as she returned to the city, she'd work out how get the statue back to the King.

She looked up, beyond the castle walls, to the distant mountains which were dark against an orange sky. Then the sun rose behind the mountains, setting the world on fire. Little by little the light slid down the walls of the castle, illuminating the world down below, until the whole oasis burst into life and light.

Slowly she released the breath she'd been holding, and rose and went into the tiled bathroom. She flicked the shower on. She couldn't let herself be seduced by this place.

She slipped off her robe. As she stepped under the deluge of warm water and slid the soap over her body, her mind drifted back of its own accord to the King. She switched the shower to cold. Nor, she reminded herself, could she allow herself to be seduced by the King. It was too risky. One misjudged comment, one guilty glance, and that would be it. She was here for one reason only, to earn enough money to get herself out of Ma'in.

*

"So, this Jabal al whatever-it-is, this treasure place. When can we go and see it?" Mahito asked. He appeared to have no problem now talking in English—the language which everyone understood.

"Jabal al Kanz. And you can't."

"Why not? If you won't renew the contract on the existing mine, won't pay us out, we'd be agreeable to transferring our interests to a new site."

"No. The land is sacred to our people."

"Sacred?" Mahito snorted. "Everyone, everything, has its price."

"Not us," Tariq replied, trying to control his anger that thudded dully in his ears. "Not Jabal al Kanz." He knew it was a risk. But it was one worth taking. Dangle the lure, and then withdraw it. It made the prey hungry, made them mad for more. More importantly, it prolonged their interest and bought him time.

Mahito leaned forward and Tariq wished he hadn't. The stale alcohol on Mahito's breath turned his stomach. "If the gold is there, like the map suggests, it'll make us both rich," he said under his breath, so only they could hear. "A win-win for both of us." He sat back and raised his voice once more to satisfy his colleagues who were leaning forward, trying to catch his whispered remarks. "Your choices are clear: pay us out, renew the original contract or show us Jabal al Kanz."

Tariq rose slowly and walked over to the screen which still showed Aurus's business presentation, his head having to move at such close quarters over the wide-framed picture to focus on the detail. Then he turned to face the meeting. "Why the haste? You have a week left of my hospitality. At the end of it, I will sign a contract, make no mistake. But, until then…" He shrugged. "There's no need to rush. Take your time. Get to know my country, the desert, in which you wish to re-invest your money."

"I think we know everything that we need to about your country. Except Jabal al Kanz." Mahito's irritation was evident in his tone and in the quick exchange of glances between him and his colleagues. He picked up a nugget of gold and brandished it triumphantly in front of the King. "It's got this. It'll make us all rich; it'll make my board happy." He looked round, grinning at the room. "What else do we need to know about Ma'in?"

"There is more to a land than the minerals it holds." Tariq didn't even try to prevent the iciness in his voice. "But we've been talking all day. It's time to call a halt to our meeting." He rose and the others followed. "We will eat outside tonight. It's been brought to my notice that you may enjoy something of the... traditional pleasures of a Bedouin meal." The men exchanged puzzled looks and Cara blushed. "Aarif will meet you in the reception hall in three hours and will show you the way."

CARA WAITED until all the men had left, except Tariq.

"Your Royal Highness—"

He glanced at her with a smile. "I thought we'd gone beyond that. Please, call me Tariq."

"*Tariq*, I hope you're not arranging this dinner because of something I said?"

Tariq continued to stare at the screen and then gave a quiet sigh and turned to Cara. "What? Oh, yes, in a way. The thought of my visitors eating in the style of my people amuses me." He turned back to the screen.

"Well, that's okay then. I guess," Cara said under her breath, not understanding in the least what Tariq was doing. She collected her things and began to move quietly away, anxious not to disturb him.

"And what do you think of this, Cara?"

She stopped in her tracks. "Your Highness?"

"These images? This... economic prize the Aurus group are so in love with. This is what they'd like to transform Jabal al Kanz into."

She walked up to him. He didn't turn around. She stood beside him and looked up at the graphs still on the screen.

"I know nothing about balance sheets."

"This is *my* country, Cara. *My* country. But this is *their* balance sheet, nothing more."

She was so struck by the passion in his voice that she

couldn't reply. She felt his emotion like a vibration running through her body, disturbing her, as it disturbed him.

"And how about this image?" he continued, flicking on to the next slide which showed the mine from a picturesque angle. Consider whether you'd like it in your own home, wherever that is—England, Italy?"

She looked from him back to the screen once more and shrugged. "It doesn't look *so* bad."

He cocked his head to one side and looked at her. "No, you're right, it doesn't." He reached over for the remote control. "How about this image?"

She gasped as a new picture flashed onto the screen.

He continued to move from one appalling image of devastation to another. "The first one was from their presentation, *their* photograph—no doubt digitally enhanced. These"—he continued to move through a stream of damning photos—"are *mine*." They stood in silence as he clicked through a procession of images which showed utter devastation.

The sun had moved away to the far side of the castle and the meeting room was shadowy and quiet. One eerie image of a land devastated by mining followed another. "It's terrible," she whispered.

"It was a beautiful land once. I was born at the old Bedouin camp now destroyed by the mining of Gold Mine I, as Aurus call it. It's real name is Jabal al Noor—Mountain of Light. It had been one of our itinerant camps since anyone could remember." He sighed and walked to the open doors around which abundant flowers climbed. He lifted his head up to a fragrant flower and pulled it down to inhale its scent. "It even appeared in our poetry. 'And fair was the land of ab Naheed, bounteous with water, with fig and date, and flower. Truly Mohammed had blessed this land that held such abundance in its hands.' The poet could not have imagined the accuracy of his words. He didn't know what lay beneath the surface. He could only see the magic shown by the sun at day, and the moon at night. A millennia of magic, destroyed in one single generation." He turned to Cara. "It's a tragic legacy to leave to my children, do you not think?" He turned suddenly and pointed to an Arabic frieze set in the stone wall. "See, there, are Naheed's words It says—"

"I know what it says." Cara could do nothing else to comfort this man, robbed of his lands, but show him she understood, even if it was only his language. "It says, 'these lands should be defended to the death, for without them, there is no life.'"

She turned triumphantly to the King and was stunned by his expression. Gone was the facade, the sadness, the arrogance. What met her gaze was the eyes of an admiring man, an equal.

"I'm not as proficient as my father but I know it enough to understand the basic meaning. But, as he was always at pains to point out, I didn't have the context to interpret it properly."

"He sounds like a hard man."

"He was strict, but not hard."

Tariq sighed. "That is a better combination than my father. He was a hard man, cruel even. But he had no discipline, no morals. So... Miss Cara Devlin, you of the clever mind and understanding nature, what would you do in my position?"

She shook her head. "I don't know."

His eyes were sad as they searched her face. "What does one do with a problem? One can ignore it or one can turn it to one's advantage." He plucked a flower and handed it to her. "Which option, Cara, do you think I've chosen?" He looked up before she could answer and nodded to Aarif, who had appeared silently behind her. "Go now. I'll see you later, at dinner. Be in the hall at seven."

It was a command and she turned and left the room, the image of the aerial photos of the open cast mines still in her mind. Open to the air, a hungry, yawning maw—a scar in the peaceful rolling desert.

This was his land and he was furious about its use—and helpless... until now.

She'd thought that he wouldn't understand anything about being used, as she and her father had been used by Piers. But he did. And on a scale that was beyond her comprehension. This wasn't a man who was going to take advantage of her, but someone who'd already been taken advantage of.

~

THERE WAS no one else in the reception hall when Cara arrived at the time Tariq had told her. She looked around the empty hall and heard footsteps approaching. Instinctively she backed toward the light from the open door. Then Tariq came into vision, his robes lightening the shadows.

"The others seem to be late," she said.

"They'll be following shortly. Aarif will escort them down." He gestured for her to go outside before him. "I wished to show you the wadi personally, without the constant interruptions of my guests who would no doubt prefer to know the value of the land per square meter, rather than appreciate its beauty."

Cara smiled. She could just picture the scene he wanted to avoid. She was also flattered. "Thank you. I've seen the trees from my room. What are they?"

"Wild pistachio trees. They grow so thickly all along the wadi, one could get lost in them. I frequently did, as a child."

He opened one of the doors in the sheltering walls of the castle and stood aside. "This way."

Immediately they were amongst the low spreading trees, their trunks covered with fissured bark, thickly leafed and abundant with pistachio nuts. They followed a winding path through them and Cara was immediately struck by a peculiar hush. They seemed miles away from the castle and the business meeting. The overhead branches caught the evening breeze and rustled, heavy with their fruit. It was the only sound. But then as they moved further down amongst the trees, she heard another sound—the sound of water flowing.

They emerged from the shady trees into an open space through which a silver streak of water moved slowly over the smooth flat stones of an ancient water course. On either side, for as far as the eye could see, the abundant trees stretched, untouched, sheltering the land.

"It's beautiful. And unexpected."

"That's Ma'in. And that's what I wish to preserve. Come, around the next bend in the river is the camp where we'll dine."

Cara listened, fascinated, not just to Tariq's description of the trees and how he was using them to bring prosperity to parts of his country. Everything about them seemed to be useful—the sap for incense, the essential oils for perfume, and their growth, to combat erosion. But what really fascinated her was Tariq's enthusiasm. Watching him look around the place he obviously loved, his face was more relaxed than she'd seen it before, and she saw him as the man, rather than the King.

"And then there's the nut itself." He stretched up and plucked one, cracked open its shell and held it out to her.

She took it and wondered why his smiled broadened. She took a bite and grimaced with disgust as she spat it out into her hand. "It tastes like turpentine!"

"Yes"—he shrugged, laughing—"the nut doesn't taste so good!"

"You might have told me." She fell into step beside him, still trying to rid herself of the taste.

He stopped walking at the curve in the river. "I might have done. But where's the fun in that?"

She tried to look stern, but suspected she didn't manage it. "Are Kings allowed to have fun?" She hadn't meant for the smile to have vanished so completely from his face.

He didn't answer, but instead pointed around the bend. She turned and saw a tent, complete with traditional Bedouin patterns, supported by date palms, like pillars, erected on a plateau beside the river. People moved around it setting out dishes of shining brass full of colorful salads, decorated with flowers of brilliant pink, red and orange, on the long, low tables, around which colorful striped sofas were arranged. The tent was open on all sides, allowing the magical atmosphere of the trees to penetrate the tent.

"Wow! Is this always here?"

"No. But I thought you might appreciate it."

She frowned. "Me, and your other guests?"

"No. You."

There was no way she could move her eyes from his. They held hers not by command, but by an interest, an intensity that was totally persuasive.

The sound of people approaching broke the spell and he looked away and sighed, his mouth turning into a grim line.

"Tariq!" Mahito called, batting away a stray branch. It cracked under his blow. Cara winced but he continued, leaving the broken branch swinging behind him.

Aarif grimaced and exchanged a glance with Tariq, whose face was hard and impassive once more. "Please come, be seated," Tariq said, gesturing to the tables. "We will be eating a traditional Zarrb Hafla this evening. The lamb has been cooking inside the earth oven over there for two hours."

"Two hours!" exclaimed Mahito. "It'll be as tough as old boots."

"It's tender, it melts in your mouth." Tariq beckoned the chef. "Please take a seat."

An hour later and Mahito had to agree. After a feast of succulent lamb, spiced Arabic salad, seasoned Bedouin rice, thick tahini, spicy matbuha, and fried eggplant with mint and cabbage with ground pepper, they were drinking Bedouin tea with baklava and fruit.

Tariq had thoughtfully placed Cara between himself and Aarif where she'd been able to enjoy the feast away from the ribald laughter and jokes of the others.

At the sound of a bird squawking close by, she excused herself and walked to the edge of the tent. It was dark beyond the lights of the tent, with only the path back to the castle lit with the occasional solar lamp. But by straining her eyes she could see the wide, slow flapping of a heavy bird flying overhead.

"It's an owl," said Tariq quietly. She hadn't realized he'd followed her. "Hunting its prey. And successful by the sound of its cry."

She turned to face him. "You've gone to a lot of trouble entertaining your guests."

"It's the Bedouin way. Entertaining is important to my people."

"Yes. But it's more than that, isn't it? You're stalling, aren't you?"

He looked at her sharply. Then sighed. "I have no choice. I apologize, Cara. You have three more days of meetings, three more days of enduring these people's"—he jerked his head behind him, indicating the men who'd somehow managed to find some whisky—"company."

"It's not all endurance," she said quietly. "Some of the time, I'm enjoying myself."

He smiled, a secret smile, all for her. "Me, too."

She swallowed and took a step away from him. "I should go now. Get an early night. More meetings to translate, you know."

He nodded slowly. "I know." He turned and waved to Aarif. "Aarif will see you back safely. Until tomorrow, then Cara."

"Until tomorrow." She smiled and walked away with Aarif, back through the quiet trees.

CHAPTER 5

Three days later

Tariq hadn't exaggerated. The meetings had continued day after day. They'd been interminable. If it hadn't been for the evenings, for the entertainment Tariq had laid on for the men, giving Tariq and Cara time to talk, the days would have dragged. Cara had begun to look forward to the evenings where Tariq would have a seat saved beside him. They'd talk of everything—politics, ideas, likes and dislikes, everything except their personal lives— things Cara needed to keep to herself. Some things she couldn't risk.

Now, the last day of the series of meetings had drawn to an early close and Cara heaved a sigh of relief. Tariq had been called away on business and she managed to slip outside without anyone noticing, needing fresh air before returning to her room to change for dinner. At least that was the end to the formal part of the week. The following day the Aurus executives were heading off for a site visit by themselves. Tariq would be away elsewhere, giving Cara a day of peace until they all met up at the palace the following day to sign the final agreement. Supposedly. Although Cara had her suspicions Tariq had something else planned.

She leaned back against the wall and inhaled the scented air and closed her eyes, focusing on the seductive trickle of the water from a fountain. She only half-listened to the men as they chatted inside the meeting room, unaware of her presence in the garden outside. They'd switched to speaking Portuguese which they hadn't done before. As it happened she knew Portuguese well, it being her mother's native tongue.

"And to think we thought this was going to be difficult, hey?" said one of the men.

"Easy!"

"We've got these Ma'inese over a barrel. They've no choice but to accept a renewed contract and the King knows it."

"But it's not as interesting as that map we saw in the Antiquities Room. If what the girl translated is correct—"

"It must be. She may not be anything to look at, but she knows her stuff."

"If the map and existing info is correct, that would be a much better proposition."

"The King would never go for it. You heard what he said… it's sacred."

"No! He wants it for himself. But he might just find he has a fight on his hands."

"What are you going to do?"

"Strategy, Atsuto, strategy. Tomorrow, the King said he won't be available. So tomorrow we go to the—what was it called? That's right, Mountain of Treasure—Jabal al Kanz, instead of Gold Mine I."

"Hey, keep your voice down. Someone might hear."

"Like one of those idiot Ma'inese. They need a translator

for Japanese. What's the chances of them knowing Portuguese?"

"True. But the translator might."

Cara opened her eyes wide but didn't move, remaining hidden behind the greenery.

"That little thing, know Portuguese? How likely is that?" They laughed. "No, that little mouse is nothing to worry about," the man huffed derisively. "Although even *she* is beginning to look attractive to me out here, in the middle of nowhere." She heard the man pace towards the window and she shrunk back further. "God, look at the place, it gives me the creeps."

"Where are the women?" Mahito continued. "The King lives like a monk and I'm not surprised, if she's an example of the women he surrounds himself with."

Cara blushed with anger and mortification while the men laughed. Despite the impulse to leave, Cara stayed put. She didn't want them to know she'd overheard—she had a feeling it would only amuse them. It hurt, of course it did. But it wasn't as if this was the first time she'd heard this kind of thing. The kind of business and political meetings she'd worked for had powerful men. And powerful men drew beautiful women to them like moths around a flame. But she'd seen enough of these powerful men to know that power was *not* an aphrodisiac for her. And she certainly wasn't an aphrodisiac for them. She lived unseen, on the edges, alone. And that was the way she preferred it. Especially now.

She closed her eyes and waited for the taunting voices to disappear. After she heard the doors close behind them, she jumped up and paced back and forth in the courtyard.

The arrogance of the men galled her. Not just their arrogant assumptions about her, but the implication that they were tricking the King. Their words played over in her mind.

Surely she must have misunderstood? She turned and paced back. No. There was nothing to misunderstand. They were after the land the King didn't want them to have, so had somehow hatched a plan to force him to release it to them.

The King was being tricked and he needed to be told. She paced back and looked inside. She should go to him now and tell him. Tomorrow could be too late.

But... she hesitated. How could she go to him? She'd always tried to make sure she was never alone with him. When she was with him she was tempted to forget everything, and *that* she could not risk.

If he knew of her connection to the ancient statue, if he knew her role, no matter how tenuous, in its theft, he'd be furious. She'd seen how much his country and his culture meant to him and she could only imagine his response if he knew she was implicated in the disappearance of the statue. He'd have her imprisoned, brought to trial for a crime she hadn't committed. She paused. But then, did he really deserve to be done over by that group of grasping businessman?

She half-turned. She owed Tariq. She owed him for all the times she'd given Piers the benefit of the doubt, for all the times she'd suppressed her better judgment because of her need to be loved, for all the times she'd compromised herself. She could change that now. She could make some small reparation to the man she and her husband had wronged.

SHE TOOK a deep breath and walked towards the wing of the castle where she knew Tariq's private quarters were.

Instinctively she stepped back into the shadows as two people emerged from a room where she heard his voice. They passed by without noticing her. Sometimes, she thought wryly to herself, it paid to go unnoticed. She stepped up to the door and froze. Her courage had held until that moment. She stepped back, her hand dropping to her side. She couldn't do it.

The door opened suddenly and he stood there. "Miss Devlin… Cara", he added more softly. "What are you doing here?" He frowned. "Did you wish to see me for some reason?"

She shook her head, suddenly losing her nerve. "No," she swallowed. "I must have … got lost." She couldn't seem to raise her eyes to his. Instead they were fixed on his exposed chest. She hadn't seen it before. It had always been covered with a robe but now he was wearing casual clothes—an open-necked shirt and trousers, and it was a shock. He'd at once become more familiar, and yet more strange, because the familiar clothes emphasized his difference. His skin was a rich nutmeg brown that seemed to invite her touch. She squeezed her hands tightly together, afraid she'd reach out to him. He slipped his hands in his trouser pockets, as if echoing her own thoughts, and planted his feet firmly apart, centering himself.

"It is not the sort of palace in which you can become lost, Cara." He opened the door wide. "Please come inside. It's been a long day, a long week I should say. Perhaps you would care for a drink while you decide whether to tell me why you're really here?" He smiled at her, a disarming smile that invited confidence. She relaxed, nodded and stepped forward, following him to a couple of settees where he indicated she should sit. "What would you like to drink?"

"Mineral water, please."

She swallowed, focusing on how the light from the lamp behind him skimmed his broad shoulders, and sat down.

He handed her the glass then stood, hands on hips, looking down at her. "So, why are you here?"

"I… I came to tell you something…"

He waited for her to continue but the longer the pause continued, the harder it became to break it. His stance was aggressive and firm, the silence practically crackled with tension. It was as if a magnet drew her eyes up to meet his. But what she saw there wasn't what she expected to see. Humor, interest and a spark of something she couldn't immediately identify.

"Is that so? You believe you have some knowledge that I do not?"

She swallowed and nodded.

"Intriguing. Please drink." He turned and walked over to the sideboard and poured himself a drink and then came and sat opposite her on a leather couch.

"So… Cara…" He paused as if he was relishing the sound of her name on his lips and looked down at his drink, swirling it around the heavy tumbler. Then he stopped swirling and the still water settled. There was a heavy pause in the air. He looked up at her suddenly. "You have a very beautiful name, you know." She could have sworn the air was sucked out of the room, depriving her of oxygen, making her forget how to breathe. His eyes hadn't left hers and she could feel herself melting under their intense, hot gaze. Then he suddenly broke it and took a drink from his glass and stood up. He strode over to the window and pushed it open. A welcome warm breeze blew in and Cara took a deep breath. "Tell me." He didn't turn around again. "What is it you have to inform me about that is so important that you'd risk your reputation by following me to my private quarters?"

She opened her mouth to speak when the meaning of his words hit her. She could feel a heavy blush flood her face. "Wait a minute! You don't believe me do you? You think I've come here for… for some *other* reason."

He still wasn't looking at her but she noticed the slight twitch of his lips as he half-turned towards her, before he placed his glass down with careful deliberation and turned back to face her, his arms crossed, but his eyes still as hot as hell. He huffed. "Come on, Cara. I know everything that's going on around here. What could you possibly tell me that I don't already know?"

Cara gulped air at his conceit. "You think I'm so insignificant that I've had no life. Certainly not worthy of a standard security check before you employed me."

"Ah, that was my brother. He was so enamored with your voice that he impulsively employed you without the usual formalities." He shrugged. "But it doesn't matter in this case." He smiled. "I hardly think you're hiding anything."

She arched an eyebrow. "Really?" She hoped the chill in her voice would pierce his cockiness. It didn't. "So you think you know all about me, then."

She watched, speechless, as he walked towards her and stopped, too close. He reached out and took her glass and set it on the table and playfully narrowed his eyes as if trying to find something he already knew. "Yes, I think I know you. Being a good judge of character is important for someone in my position."

She rose and folded her arms defensively. "Okay, so tell me all about me. I'd love to hear what you think."

He shrugged. "Where shall I begin? Perhaps your personal life. You live alone. There is no man in your life."

She bit the inside of her lip. Was it so obvious that she was useless at relationships? "Do carry on. I'm finding this enlightening. The fact that I was able to come here at extremely short notice would suggest I have no significant other." She tried to keep her face neutral but somehow she doubted she'd succeeded, if his smug expression was anything to go by.

"And… you're strong, but you don't know it, because you haven't given yourself a chance to find out."

His eyes had turned softer now. The brown was melting, like chocolate on a hot day. It aroused her senses in much the same way. She wanted to taste him. "I…"

"You… should leave now, before I say something"—he reached out and pushed a stray strand of hair back from her face—"or *do* something we'll both regret."

She swallowed, trying to control her body's reaction to his touch. She shook her head. Or she meant to. But it hardly moved. Instead she felt his hand sweep her cheek, instead of her hair. She looked up into eyes that were warmer, if that were possible. She opened her mouth to speak but nothing emerged.

"You should go now," he repeated. But his eyes were telling her to stay. His hands came up either side of her and he dipped his head towards her. She saw the flare of his nostrils as he inhaled a deep breath, his nose close to her cheek, nearly touching her. Then he pulled away, his eyes searching her face. "You're not moving. Don't you realize it's dangerous for you here? Don't you believe what people say about me? Aren't you worried you've come to find the ogre, the '*wahs*' people describe me as?"

She shook her head. Swallowed once more. "No."

"Then you're crazy. You should listen to these men. Why don't you believe them?"

"Because I trust my own instincts more."

"Is that so? And what are your instincts telling you now?"

"That you aren't an ogre. You only think you are."

His hand froze on her cheek and he looked into her eyes. The veil of kingship fell, revealing the man she'd seen the night they'd walked through the trees.

"You're wrong. I *am* that ogre. And only a fool would believe otherwise."

She took his hand and pulled it away from her face. "Then I am *that* fool. They may think you're an ignorant monster but I don't believe you are. For some reason that I don't understand, you've allowed these men to believe this. And you're delaying signing the contract. You won't sign it because you know it's not in your interests to sign. And…"

"Yes?"

"The men have no intention of visiting the site tomorrow. They've arranged instead to go to Jabal al Kanz. It seems they paid handsomely for their guide's silence."

He merely nodded. She couldn't read his face. "Anything else?"

"Yes, actually. The 'treasure' I translated. It was nagging at my mind. It has another meaning." She paused, but he didn't speak. "It also means 'water.'"

"You're clever, Cara, but unfortunately your knowledge has failed you on that point."

"But—"

He shook his head. "You contradict me? The King of this country? You think you know my language better than I do?"

"No, of course not. It's just—"

"Good. You don't understand me or my country or the issues at stake. And I don't expect you to. But I thank you for your courage."

"Courage?"

"Yes. It took courage to seek me out and tell me your suspicions. I appreciate that." He hesitated. "Very much. Now go."

She nodded, unreasonably disappointed. She'd done all this and yet he'd simply dismissed her, and her suspicions, like that? She'd thought he was different, that he'd listen to her. She wanted to go—leave then and there—and forget about Tariq, about Ma'in, about everything.

"Just a few more days. And then this will all be over."

Was he reading her mind? "A few more days. So… you'll sign the contract then?"

"You question me, the King?" His voice was suddenly chilly and distant.

"No, forgive me, Your Highness."

There was a long pause and when she looked up she saw his eyes were warm again. "Where did the first name basis go? Ah, yes, it went when I pulled rank. But Cara, there is nothing to forgive. And yes, it will all be over by the end of the week."

She nodded and stepped through the door he opened for her. It was only as she was walking away that she realized he hadn't answered her question about the contract.

Tariq was seldom surprised by anything or anyone. But, as he sat back in his chair, flicked on the bank of cameras and watched her disappear down the corridor to her room, he realized that Cara had succeeded in doing just that. Not just surprising him, but enticing him further. It was as if she held a skein of fine silk—strong and unbreakable—with which she was winding him closer to her.

He'd never seen a woman with such courage and integrity. That she should step out of the professional world of which she was a part, and have the courage to come to him, astounded him. She had no vested interest in what she told him. She had no connection to him. But she came anyway, risking his displeasure, risking discovery by the others.

He watched her disappear from sight and closed his eyes. The strength had been there all the time, in the set of her slim shoulders, straight as a die and firm against everything, but he'd not seen it immediately. Like everything else about her, she seemed to reveal herself little by little. He wondered what else he'd discover if he allowed himself to get to know her more.

He closed the door and walked to his desk and called Aarif, who appeared instantly.

"Change of plan. Miss Devlin won't be accompanying our guests to the site." He paused as he remembered the slight sway of her hips as she'd walked off down the corridor, the brief penetrating glance of her eyes, and that voice... always that voice. He wondered how he could have been so wrong. And not just him, but every man in this castle. They'd all taken her at face value. None of them had been able to see the steely core hidden inside her. And her cleverness. Not one in a thousand scholars would have come up with the correct, alternative translation of the word 'treasure'. And his under-estimation of her could cost him dearly. He still hadn't received word from Sahmir. He still had to stall the Aurus executives, and their interest in Jabal al Kanz was his best bet. He couldn't risk her telling the Aurus executives her doubts.

"Sir?" Aarif prompted.

Tariq glanced back at his assistant. "Miss Devlin will be coming with me to Qawaran and from there, to the city. Not tomorrow, but immediately. See that she's ready to leave within the hour."

CHAPTER 6

Five minutes had passed and the King had barely said a word. Not that Cara wanted one word, she thought angrily. She expected more than that. She expected a proper explanation for why he'd commanded—for there could be no other word to describe his 'request'—her presence on an apparently scheduled trip to a neighboring country.

She continued to gaze studiously out the window of the small two-seater plane as it flew over miles of rolling desert.

Against all reason to the contrary, she had no fear that he was making off with her for nefarious reasons of his own. She wasn't the kind of woman men made off with. No, his assistant had muttered something about Qawaran translation. It was simply a job. So why the secrecy?

Despite her annoyance, Cara had never seen anything quite so beautiful in all her life. The land stretched on for what looked like an eternity to a horizon of undulating charcoal, stark against a massive sky. They continued to climb in the small aircraft until Qusayr Zarqa grew tiny. As if waiting for a sign, Tariq turned the plane into a smooth twist and, with the sun behind them, they turned away from the desert castle and headed toward the mountains.

Still seething at his peremptory tone when he'd greeted her, she listened to him complete his exchange with ground control—whoever and wherever they were in this empty land. He flicked a control and the static went quiet.

"I apologize for the sudden invitation, Cara."

She swung around to face him. "Invitation? I didn't realize I had a choice."

He smiled that warm smile that he kept so hidden. It reached his eyes in a sign of genuine amusement.

"You are correct to be irritated. Even though"—he shrugged, still smiling—"I *am* the King. Even if people are irritated, they usually hide it, but I doubt you could hide anything, could you?"

She closed her eyes briefly as the irony of his comment hit home. She was hiding the biggest secret of her life from him. "I haven't forgotten who you are, Your Royal Highness—"

"Cara! Call me Tariq."

"Tariq. So… am I allowed to know why you've ordered me into the sky at night?

"It's not yet night—the sun is still high in the sky. You're still able to see what I wish you to see."

She frowned. "You want *me* to see something? Why? I'm just the translator."

"You're not *just* anything, Cara. I wish you to see something so you'll understand." He paused, looked out the window and re-gripped the controls. "I *want* you to understand. There." He pointed. "Down there."

She looked down and saw a dark scar in the desert that opened up under them like an angry sore on unblemished skin. Her anger vanished, consumed by appalled awe at the devastation unfolding beneath them. At the centre of the vast open cast mine, the land fell away in deep rifts between the rocky strata that lay beneath the sand.

"That's the mine Aurus has had control of, isn't it?"

"Yes. The Aurus Group's legacy to my country, which my father sanctioned. Of course, he didn't know the devastation it would cause. But then, he had little interest. He wanted progress at any cost."

"It looks terrible."

"And it's not just cosmetic. The mine demolished ancient settlements, diverted waterways that once irrigated crops and changed the landscape."

"I had no idea."

"Few people do. The mine's a long way from anywhere now, and highly automated."

Silence settled between them as they flew over the blasted site, toward the mountains. Only once they'd left the area and the land had changed from rolling sand dunes to stony hammada plains did Cara sit back in her seat.

"I'm sorry."

He glanced at her. "Why should you be sorry? It's a well-kept secret unless you have a vested interest in plundering my country of its treasure." He smiled at her. "Which I assume you don't."

It was like a knife entering a wound that now had no defenses. Except she didn't hurt for *her*. She hurt for *him*.

She reached out and covered his hand that was loosely over the controls with her own. She had no words to give him, only her touch. He exhaled roughly and shook his head revealing the despair, of which she now understood some small part.

"At least down there"—she pointed to a wooded area—"your land is regenerating."

"Indeed. Except we are no longer in my country."

She looked out the window. Nothing had changed. "Where are we?"

"In Qawaran. Tonight you will meet my close friends and neighbors, the Kings of Qawaran and Sitra and their families. As small neighboring countries we work closely together. I think you will like them."

Cara blinked in wonder. She was sure they were nice people if Tariq said so. But that he would take the trouble to introduce her—a mere translator—to them, and that he'd also be interested whether she would like them or not, astounded her. Yes, she was sure she'd like a couple of royal families, each with lives so different to her own. But what would they think of her?

THE PALACE EMERGED from a rock face, forming soaring walls that tumbled down the mountain side and into the desert. It was like a city. Like Tariq's desert palace, there was no doubt it was originally a desert stronghold—a fortress to repel invaders. It was the only habitation for miles.

Tariq expertly landed the plane on a small airstrip in the desert and by the time they exited the plane, a car had already approached from the Palace, dust blooming in its wake. As they walked toward the car, two women stepped out with two men close behind them. The two women were both blondes, one tall and willowy and one shorter wearing a big smile.

"Tariq!" called the tall woman. "This is an unexpected pleasure!"

The two men arrived and greeted Tariq.

"Lucky for you that we're all still here"—called the shorter woman, walking up to Tariq and giving him an unceremonious hug—"we're off early tomorrow." Much to Cara's surprise Tariq didn't push her away. He looked happy to see her.

"Lucky for me you're still here, indeed, Lucy, because otherwise you would never forgive me."

"Yeah, you got it. We're going to a wedding tomorrow, leaving before sunrise. You could have come after all, Tariq!"

Tariq turned to the taller woman. "Anna! Good to see you again. Sorry for the short notice." He gave her a hug and then turned to Cara as the two Kings stood before her, tall and regal.

Looking at the imposing man in front of her she didn't know whether to curtsey, shake his hand, or run away. Luckily he knew what to do. "Welcome to Qawaran. It is a great pleasure to receive a friend Tariq's. We don't often get the chance."

"You bet," said the tall blonde walking beside him. He put his arm around the woman who melted into his side. "And in case my husband hasn't introduced himself he's Zahir, sheikh of this place, and I'm Anna. And this is Lucy and Razeen. It's a real pleasure to meet you."

Cara was confused. She narrowed her eyes against the brightness of both the light and this beautiful blonde. "I'm the translator. Tariq hired me for his business meeting."

If Cara had hopes that this explanation would settle matters she was let down. Because there was a chorus of knowing "Ohs", and a few grins as they exchanged looks while Tariq finished with the airplane and joined them.

"This is Miss Devlin. Cara Devlin. She's my interpreter."

Much to Cara's surprise, Lucy playfully punched Tariq in the chest. "And you need an interpreter, why exactly?"

King Zahir, obviously feeling that things were becoming too flippant turned to Cara. "You are most welcome, Miss Devlin. My wife will show you to your room."

Lucy hooked an arm through Cara's. "You're just in time for dinner."

The three men walked ahead of them into the compound, across the startling white courtyard, and Cara paused, looking up all around her at the impressive building. It was very old and yet beautifully maintained; signs of the ancient Bedouin culture were everywhere. It melded seamlessly into the rock face, high above which hawks soared. It was a place of grandeur, and beauty—and as alien as hell.

"So, Tariq, my friend." Zahir signaled for coffee while Tariq and Razeen made themselves comfortable on the oversized suede sofas. "How are your negotiations proceeding with the Aurus Group? Do you have them where you want them yet?"

Tariq accepted a coffee and sat back, enjoying being in the company of people who understood his life more completely than anyone else. "Not yet. But I will."

"Best case scenario?" asked Razeen, who was accustomed to a less autocratic rule than Zahir, and so could better appreciate the delicacy of the situation.

"Sahmir gets the investors and funds to pay Aurus off and we regain control of our land. I'll divert the river back to its original course and use the mine as a reservoir to irrigate the land, bring it back to what it was."

"What are the odds on that?"

"Slim. I'm delaying them as much as I can to give Sahmir time. And I've had some help from an unexpected quarter."

"And you say there's nothing we can do to help?"

"Thank you for your offers. It's enough to know you're behind me. But the CEO refuses to be strong-armed, so I'm taking a different approach." Tariq smiled. "A much more subtle approach."

"Intriguing."

Tariq took a sip of coffee, relishing its bitter-sweet taste. "She is."

Cara only had time for a quick shower and change of clothes before there was a knock at her door.

To her surprise, when she opened it, Anna and Lucy stood outside.

"My husband has already commandeered Tariq for a meeting and apparently they don't need you to translate!" Anna smiled wryly. "Fancy a drink?"

"Sure, thanks." Cara wondered how she should address these two women, who despite appearances, were royal. "Your Royal High—"

Anna waved her hand dismissively. "Oh, you don't have to bother with all that. Just call me Anna."

"You can call me 'Your Royal Highness', if you like," grinned Lucy. "I quite like it. No one else calls me that."

"Because you tell them not to. And you spend your days with people out in the real world. *And*, because you're the most informal person I know."

"True," said Lucy, adopting a thoughtful pose. "Us Kiwis are all pretty informal and democratic."

"You're a New Zealander?" asked Cara as she stepped out into the ancient corridor.

"Originally. Then I became a citizen of the world and now I'm a Sitran." They fell into step. She flashed a brilliant smile at Cara. "And what brings you to Ma'in? You're English, aren't you?"

"Yes. I came here first with my parents—must have been about five years ago. My father was a visiting professor at the university. After the death of my parents, well, I guess you could say I've been traveling ever since."

"No ties to return to in England?"

AWAKENED BY THE SHEIKH

Cara shook her head. "Only distant relatives."

"Good."

Anna and Lucy exchanged quick glances.

"Why 'good?'"

"Because that means you'll stay. Tariq never turns up with a woman. And I mean *never*."

Cara was flattered. Then she frowned. "I'm a translator. He's hired me to be here."

"See any translation going on?" asked Lucy with a laugh.

Cara smiled briefly, uncertain as to Tariq's motives.

"Cara," Anna said as if reading her mind, "Tariq is one of the most upright men I know. He's brought you here because he genuinely likes you and wants to spend time with you. Not to *use* you, for translating or anything else. That's just not his style."

Cara must have looked amazed at Anna's perceptive comment because Lucy gave Anna a proud hug. "You get used to Anna reading your mind. It's what makes her the best lawyer in the country, or probably any country." Lucy laughed. "Anyhow, we're glad you're going to stick around Ma'in. It'll mean we can see more of you."

"Oh, no, I'm not staying. That's impossible."

The women stared at her. "Why?" they asked in unison, as if unable to imagine any reason why a woman would want to leave this land, Tariq, or them.

"Because I'm leaving soon."

"But I thought you had no ties anywhere?"

"I don't. It's just that… I've decided to move to Italy."

"Italy?" they both exclaimed.

Cara shrugged. "It's warm, it doesn't rain, I know the language a little and… it's somewhere new."

Anna placed a hand on Cara's arm and they all stopped walking. They were standing in the middle of a large space, walls inset with ancient mosaics. "You do what you have to do, Cara. God knows, life isn't easy and Zahir and my start to life together was rocky. Put it this way, the "wedded" bit of "wedded bliss" came first by a long chalk."

"And now," grinned Lucy, "it's all bliss."

Anna raised an eyebrow and smiled enigmatically. "Something like that."

"A *lot* like that from what I hear. Come on, let's go and get that drink. It'll soon be time for dinner and we won't be able to talk about the men then! Besides, our children are dying to meet you."

"Children?"

"We've three each," said Lucy. "Anna claims she's stopping at three but there's no way I am." She patted a slightly swollen stomach. "Number four on its way and then… who knows. I was never very good at math."

Under the shade of a spreading tree, snacks of hummus, pitas, pickles, olives and stuffed vine leaves as well as other sundry tempting dishes were laid out on a table, beside sweet smelling herbals teas and juices. All around the courtyard, water flowed in geometric channels, fed from the mountain stream. Cara thought how lucky Lucy and Anna were, to be so happy and content. Anna had referred to a rocky start to her marriage but Cara couldn't believe that life had ever been anything other than rosy for either woman. They were both far too beautiful, accomplished, too bright and charming to have ever had to endure hardship.

A COUPLE of hours later and Cara realized how wrong she'd been. Lucy and Anna might be all of those things she'd imagined, but that hadn't made their life easy, far from it. But they'd come through and that gave Cara hope.

She'd also learned more about Tariq than she'd gleaned

from her time living in Ma'in and a week in his company. The women described a man who'd had a difficult life married to a woman who had been entirely unsuited to him. It had been what Anna and Lucy *hadn't* said about his wife, who had tragically died young, that had been so informative. Both were too nice to speak ill of the dead, but it was obvious the marriage had been arranged with only politics in mind, not Tariq's happiness.

And, she'd got to meet all of their children. The children all knew each other well and treated each other as siblings, even if they weren't. But they were obviously the next best thing. It was in the interests of each of the three relatively small countries to work closely together which meant they saw each other often.

Anna glanced at her watch. "Kids!" she called with her honeyed American accent. "Time for bed."

The eldest appeared at her side. "But mama, surely I don't have to go. I'm not a baby any more."

Anna rose and gave the tall, gangly pre-teen a hug. "You'll always be my baby, Matta. But no, you don't have to leave. You may dine with us tonight."

Matta seemed to grow a couple of inches in delight as he assumed the role of elder brother and made sure the rest of the children were packed off to bed with their respective nurses.

Cara stepped up beside Anna, following her gaze as Matta dealt with the other children.

"He's a handsome boy. He's going to be tall."

"Yeah. Like his father."

Cara knew from the tabloids that Matta had been born while Anna had been married to Zahir's brother, Abduallah. She also knew that Abduallah was a lot shorter than Zahir, but Anna said nothing. It seemed Cara wasn't the only one with secrets.

They walked into the dining room and were greeted by the men who entered through the main door.

"Ladies!" King Zahir's voice boomed out.

All three men were equally tall and commanding but there was something about Zahir which was positively unnerving. His tone could have been commanding, scolding or welcoming, she had no idea. But Anna did.

While Matta joined Razeen and Lucy by the window to look out at the hawks being exercised, Anna walked up to Zahir and it was as if a light flashed on inside him as he wrapped one arm around her and drew her to him, tilted her chin upwards and kissed her. Anna placed a hand on his chest to push him away but the flat of her hand turned into a grip as she gathered the cloth of his robes in her hand, as if she wanted to press her fingers into his flesh. The grip, and her suddenly flushed face, betrayed the fact that pushing him away was the last thing she wanted to do.

He smiled, the triumphant smile of a man who knows he has the undivided attention of his woman, and caressed her cheek, dipped his mouth to her ear and whispered something. Whatever his words, Anna's flush deepened, she inhaled slowly, as if trying to steady herself and Cara half-turned away, appalled by the feeling of envy that consumed her. Even her husband who she had no doubt had been fond of her once, had never looked at her that way. But before she could walk away, someone touched her arm. It was too light at touch to have made as big an impact as it did. She looked up into Tariq's eyes. He dipped his head to hers.

"Zahir and Anna have always been unable to conceal their passion for each other," he observed in a low voice. "It can make one feel a little uncomfortable until one becomes accustomed to it."

"I didn't feel uncomfortable. I felt…" She stopped, realizing that the thoughts she'd been trying to form in her mind would be too revealing.

"What did you feel?"

She shook her head, unable to speak. How could she tell him a truth so personal? And yet she couldn't lie to him.

Although they weren't touching, she felt more intimate with him there, in this strange castle, overlooking the wide plains, with the low apricot beams of sunset streaming in through the arched stone windows. "I'd know what you feel, Cara." The breeze tossed a strand of hair onto her cheek. He pushed it away. "I'd like to know everything about you. Because, the more time I spend with you, the more I realize there *is* to know. You're deceptive. So much lying behind that calm, unassuming façade."

She shook her head, trying to negate his words, while at the same time being sucked helplessly under the current of his allure. She wanted what Anna had—that passion that consumed everything. And she felt it when Tariq was near. She swallowed. "I'm just me. Don't think there's more than there is."

To her consternation, he smiled. "That's just what I'd expect you to say. So, tell me, what did you think when Zahir kissed Anna?"

"I thought she was lucky to have someone who adores her like Zahir obviously does."

He nodded. "Indeed. Such love is rare in marriage, I think. Rare, but not impossible. Maybe it means one should accept how one feels, even if one finds such passion in the most unexpected places." He dipped his head to hers and she held her breath. "Come, let's go and join Razeen and Lucy. Their love is equally strong, but maybe a little more sociable."

She followed him to the window where hawks made a magical sight swooping and soaring in the waning light, catching the wind eddies high above them where the castle disappeared into the craggy rocks, and for once in her life she felt elated, and she felt she was in the right place, at the right time, with the right person.

Cara enjoyed the evening far more than she had expected to. Zahir's sisters and eldest children also joined them. While the dining room was suitably royal and imposing, the company was relaxed and the conversation easy, as with a big family. Tariq had been placed opposite Cara and he explained any in-jokes to her, and made sure that she was always included in the conversation, for which she was grateful, if not surprised. There was no one at dinner who required her language skills and Cara was beginning to wonder whether Anna and Lucy weren't correct. Tariq had brought her here as a friend, not as an employee. In which case, what exactly was he expecting from her? As the evening drew to a close, she knew she'd find out.

She looked up, suddenly aware that she'd been lost in her own thoughts and that now there was a pause in the conversation and people were looking at her.

"I don't know," replied Tariq to some question. "You'll have to ask Cara."

He took a sip of his drink, but his eyes never left hers, his mouth unsmiling.

"Have to ask Cara what?" She smiled sociably at Lucy.

"I was just saying to Tariq that I hope we'll be seeing more of you. You should both come to Sitra next month. We're celebrating the opening of a fleet of mobile pediatric units."

Razeen smiled at Cara, whose confusion was obviously apparent. "It also happens to be a significant anniversary in my country's history but my wife prefers to celebrate advances in women's and children's health rather than the number of years my family have been the crowned rulers of the country."

"I prefer doing something real, something that makes a difference to people," remonstrated Lucy.

"And that my love"—Razeen picked up her hand and kissed it, his admiration obvious—"is one of the reasons why I love you so much."

Lucy shook her head, but was unable to prevent a smile. "You're such a smooth talker, Razeen." The smile turned into a laugh, as she turned once more to Cara. "Anyway, there'll be celebrations and it would be wonderful if you would join us all."

Razeen gave Lucy a warning glance, but Lucy ignored him. It seemed even royalty could be over-ruled by a strong-willed woman. Particularly if the King in question was obviously head-over-heels in love with that woman.

"I…" She didn't know how to respond. They were all giving her the role of a much closer friend than she was to Tariq. Her cheeks burned with embarrassment.

"Wouldn't it Tariq?" pressed Lucy, obviously used to getting her own way.

Cara couldn't bring herself to look at Tariq. But she could feel his eyes upon her. "Of course," he said. "Cara, it would be my pleasure to take you to Sitra, if you're able to come." She looked up at him from beneath lowered lashes, biting her lip, unsure of what was happening. "I would like it if you would come," Tariq clarified.

"I… I'm not sure. I have other plans. England, to wind up some business matters, and then I'm moving to Italy."

"You have pressing business there?" Lucy asked.

"Well, no. But…"

"It's up to you, Cara." Tariq's voice was gentle and persuasive. "But I would be honored if you'd be my guest at the palace and travel to Sitra."

She found herself nodding, despite the nagging voice inside her telling her she had to stay away from him. A part of her cut off that voice of sense, and she heard herself say, 'yes'. There was something totally compelling about him.

"Good," he said.

"Then that's settled," said a triumphant Lucy.

"Have you been up to your mischief-making again?" called Anna from down the other end of the table.

The dinner had finished and Lucy rose. "Just making the world a happier place, Anna. You know me!"

Cara rose too and excused herself. She went to the bathroom and splashed cold water on her face, looking up at eyes that were bright and excited. She hardly recognized herself. Just the thought of Tariq made her stomach flip and melt with desire. Was this simply lust or something more? She didn't know. She'd always said she could never trust another man, but with each day she knew Tariq, she was trusting him more and more.

She slipped quietly into the hall and was about to walk into the courtyard outside the dining room when she heard voices. She paused behind a screen.

"You like her, don't you?" she heard Lucy ask Tariq.

"Mind you own business, Lucy," Razeen interjected.

"Cara's tried to tell us she's here as translator, but she's more than that to you, isn't she?" Lucy wouldn't be put off. "You like her."

"Lucy, you're being rude."

"No, I'm not. Tariq's like the big brother I never had. You know not to take offense, eh, Tariq?"

Tariq sighed. "Lucy, you're incorrigible. And I doubt I will ever take offense at what you say, because you are one of the kindest people I know, *okhti*."

"You see!" Lucy said to Razeen. "He doesn't mind, he calls me his sister, he *gets* me. I just like people to be happy. I just want *Tariq* to be happy. He's been unhappy for too long—"

"I haven't!"

"And Cara makes you happy, doesn't she?" Lucy continued, ignoring Tariq's reply.

There was a pause and Cara strained to her Tariq's reply. Then it came, low and resonant. "Yes. Yes, she does."

Cara stepped backwards, needing to be alone, needing to process what she'd just heard. She walked away, back to the dining room. But any thoughts of being alone were thwarted by the presence of Razeen, who had returned to collect something for Lucy.

"Cara, you look as if you've seen a ghost. Is everything all right?"

She nodded. "Yes, sorry, just tired, I guess. It's been a long day."

"And I'm sure my wife's clumsy, but well-intentioned matchmaking skills haven't helped. I'm sorry about that." He paused. "Why not retire early?"

"I don't want to appear rude."

"You won't. Despite being the so-called 'Desert Kings', we're an understanding group."

They walked back to the courtyard where Razeen saved Cara any difficulty. "I told Cara she should go to bed, she looks exhausted."

Anna and Lucy looked anxiously at Cara. "Are you okay?"

"Yes, just tired."

"Sure," Anna said. "Look, you must come back to visit. We're all off early tomorrow morning so we won't see you again this time. But don't be a stranger."

Cara smiled, wondering how on earth she could casually visit the King and Queen of Qawaran. "That would be lovely."

"I'll show you to your room."

But before they could leave Tariq stepped forward. "I'll show her. Her room is in the same wing as mine."

Cara couldn't remonstrate because she knew she needed someone to show her. The palace was huge and she had no idea how to get back to her room. She needed someone's help. She'd just have preferred it to be anyone but Tariq.

If there were any questions as to Tariq's motive, no one was rude enough to reveal them either in their expression or what they said as they returned to their conversations after bidding Cara their final farewells.

"You are truly well, Cara?" Tariq asked.

"Yes, just tired. I'll be fine tomorrow."

"Then come, I'll show you the way."

It was as if Cara had stepped back in time. The ancient hallways, with their soaring arches and worn stone pathways, must have been exactly as they were in medieval times. Parts of the palace were still untouched by electricity. And, when they walked down those corridors, torches lit the way, thrust in sconces, darting out their light on stray night breezes. It was magical. And walking beside this man, whose words to Lucy still lingered in Cara's mind, made her feel even more unreal.

He stopped walking. "Cara." He spoke softly but still his voice carried around the large space.

She stopped walking and turned to him, all her senses on edge.

"Good night." He stepped away and instinctively she stepped towards him.

"You're leaving?" she asked before she could stop herself.

He smiled and opened a door. "Your room is here. Thank you for coming with me tonight. I know it makes little sense to you, but I'm glad you came."

"Why?"

"It's so rare I can be with someone I trust instinctively

and absolutely." He reached for her hand and kissed it. "Sleep well." He turned and walked away.

She went inside and closed the door and leaned back against it. She held the hand he'd kissed, still feeling the brush of his lips against her skin.

She had to tell him about the statue. He said he trusted her. But what was more important? That she should assuage her guilt and tell him the truth, in which case he'd never want to see her again, or that she should continue to fool him into believing a false version of herself?

CHAPTER 7

Despite the luxurious surroundings, Cara tossed and turned all night. She finally awoke in the early morning and, with absolute clarity, knew what she'd do. She'd tell him.

She was awake before dawn, having heard Anna and Lucy and their families leave the palace, bound for the Bedouin wedding. Impulsively, she put on a dress that had been her mother's that she'd always intended to wear, but never had. It was a dress the color of sunrise, a million miles from her usual quiet clothes. But she needed courage this morning. There was no one around except for the servants when she ventured forth into the palace. They told her that King Tariq was in the guest library.

She followed directions to the library—if this was the guest library, the main one must be huge—but it was empty. She looked around the room. His laptop and papers lay on the desk, together with a half-drunk cup of coffee. She was drawn to the open doors, beyond which, amongst the palm trees and other greenery, was a patch of vivid blue, another fountain no doubt. Perhaps he, too, had been tempted into the garden by the soothing sound of the water and the fragrance of the flowers.

She wandered along the path that led down through the private gardens. A warm breeze blew through the clattering palms until the patch of blue was revealed to be a swimming pool, shady and inviting under a pergola, fed from the water descending from the mountain, through rills and fountains, down into the pool and then beyond.

The pool was rippled, the gentle waves arrowing to a 'V' but there was no sign of the person who'd just left the pool. She was about to turn away when she heard the music. The elegant strains of Mozart's Adagio in E for violin, floated across the air, taking her back to her childhood. She smiled and hardly knowing what she was doing, found the source of the music in a summer house where pool essentials were kept. She walked up to the speaker with the phone attached and tapped the screen, checking the name of the violinist. It was her mother.

She leaned back against the wall, suddenly feeling weak, and closed her eyes. The music soared and swept through the warm air, penetrating her defenses. She hadn't been expecting it, had never listened to her mother's music since her death. God knows how she managed to avoid it, but she had. And here, miles from anywhere under the hot desert sky, it got to her, driving the pain of her loss deep into her heart.

With her eyes closed tight she could see the swing and thrust of her mother's arm moving the bow against the strings with a sensitivity she'd always shown with Cara. She could feel the way her mother's hand had swept her cheek after she'd kissed her goodnight, every night her mother had been alive. She'd only outlived her father by a few weeks. Accidental drowning the police had said. And that's what Cara wanted to believe. But, in her heart, she knew it had been no accident. Her mother simply hadn't wanted to go on living without her husband.

She didn't know how long she'd stood there, weak, against the wall, tears tracking down hot cheeks from beneath eyes squeezed tight, but the long piece eventually drew to an end.

The reality of the world that surrounded her slowly filtered into her consciousness once more. The clatter of the palms that surrounded the pool outside, the light breeze shifting the sheer gauzy curtains across the tiled floor. And something else… She wiped her eyes with the palms of her hands and turned to walk away. But someone was coming. She'd only just reached the door when he spoke.

"Cara! Have you come to swim?"

She didn't turn around immediately, knowing the grief was still too evident in her eyes, the tears still fresh on her face. "No, I don't swim. I don't like water. I… I must have taken the wrong turn."

"You were looking for me, I think?"

His voice was soft, so gentle it turned the knife in the wound that hearing her mother's violin had opened up. She couldn't help prevent a sob from rising through her body and it escaped her mouth in a gasp. She clamped her hand against her mouth, but it was too late.

He was beside her immediately. "What is it? What's the matter?"

There was concern in his voice and it only made things worse. She bowed her head and swiped her eyes with her hands. She looked up at the ceiling and willed the tears to stop. She shook her head again. "Nothing," she whispered.

"Turn around."

He was sheikh, he was King and he wasn't used to having an order refused. And part of her wanted comfort and couldn't refuse. She turned around. He frowned, and lifted her chin as he looked into her eyes.

"You're crying. Are you hurt?" His eyes suddenly blazed. "Has someone hurt you?"

She shook her head in confusion. His eyes held a dark fury. "No." She shook her head again. "No," more firmly this time.

"Then what has brought these tears to your eyes?"

"Something personal. I can't explain."

"Come, take a seat. Drink?"

Again she had no thought of not complying. Somehow she imagined he would be as commanding even if he weren't king. She sat on the sofa and watched as he walked to the drinks cabinet and poured them both sparkling water. He had nothing but swim shorts on and his broad, muscled body was revealed in all its power. A rivulet of water suddenly fell from his hair and snaked its way down the dark skin of his back before being absorbed into the wet shorts, shorts that molded to his body.

She swallowed and looked away. He turned and brought the drinks over to her. The diversion of his semi-naked body had helped her to recover more swiftly than anything else could.

He put the drinks on the table and sat opposite her. "Now tell me what happened. You're not the type of woman who would be upset by trivialities."

She raised her eyebrows involuntarily. He was spot on. She wasn't sentimental. She was always at pains *not* to feel. Music was one of the few things that short-cut her defense mechanisms. But, however perceptive he was, however powerful, she wasn't one of his subjects, wasn't going to open up to him simply because he demanded her to.

She took a sip of her water and cleared her throat. "I'm

fine really. It was just a silly memory that upset me for a moment."

His frown deepened. "So nothing happened to upset you?"

She shrugged, a smile slipping onto her lips. "No, I'm not upset easily."

"Is that so?" A smile flickered on his lips. "You're too hard, maybe?"

She huffed a brief laugh and took a sip of her drink.

He sat back, staring at her thoughtfully. "No, I know you're not."

She looked up to find his eyes staring into hers. "You don't know me."

"I don't need to hear people say they are one thing, or the other, to believe or not believe. I can see it in their eyes, how their body moves, what they *don't* say as much as what they *do* say." He pursed his lips and swilled his drink around, before looking up at her once more. "No, you're not hard. What you *are* is intelligent and strong. You know who you are and don't let other people's ignorant, uninformed opinions affect you."

She blinked at the accuracy of his statement. Then frowned, confused, both by his words and that he should have thought about her at all. She opened her mouth to speak but found the words had evaporated into thin air.

He smiled briefly, frowning himself now, and sat back. "So, what is it that brings tears to your eyes?" She glanced at the music and he followed her eyes. "I left the music on. Now, it's off. Did you turn it off?"

She nodded, a hard little ball beginning to form in her chest as she thought of her mother's music once more. The silence lengthened between them. She swallowed the hard ball down and turned to him with a brightness she didn't feel. He'd know it was false but it was the best she could do.

"My mother. She was a musician. It was her music you were playing."

If she hadn't been looking into his eyes she would never have believed that an expression could change so quickly. One minute his eyes had been commanding, probing, intense. But in the second it takes for a desert evening to turn into a darkness full of mystery and magic, his eyes darkened, melted with an emotion she'd not seen before in him.

"Your mother…" he said softly, nodding. "She's passed away?"

She nodded, unable to speak.

He held her gaze for a few long moments, the melting chocolate of his eyes caressing and comforting her although they were seated apart. Then he rose and walked over to the music. He prodded at the screen and read through the list. "Joanna Devlin, the violinist. She is… *was* a gifted musician. I understand now."

She glanced at him and realized he did understand. He didn't have to utter words of consolation, platitudes to communicate his sympathy and understanding. It was there in his manner, in his eyes, in the undeniable connection they shared.

"And have you inherited your mother's gifts?"

"No. I don't play an instrument."

"You have your languages and your voice, Cara. You make magic with your voice."

She stepped away. It was getting too intense. She had to go.

"I'm sorry, I've intruded. I should be going."

"Wait." He placed his hand lightly on her arm but it felt as if she couldn't move unless he lifted it. "You came here for a reason, Cara." The sound of her name on his lips slipped over his tongue like a caress. "Why? Why did you come here?"

She should tell him. Tell him now. Tell him that she'd betrayed him and his country, by not questioning her husband about his activities, by allowing him full access to her and her father's research files. She'd known something had been going on but she hadn't wanted to know for sure.

But Tariq's hand still rested on her arm and the surge of blood through her veins it prompted made her feel more alive than she'd ever felt before. Perhaps she didn't need to tell him yet. Besides, she had to return to the city and he was her only way back. If she told him he'd never speak to her again. If she didn't tell him, she could enjoy his company for the last few days of her contract and then return to the city and return the statue to him.

It was a plan and one her body was anxious for her to accept.

"Something pressing to tell me?" He smiled as if certain she hadn't. If only he knew. If only she could tell him. "You're silent, Cara. I have been killing time, swimming, trying to get you out of my mind. Waiting until breakfast when I could reasonably see you again."

She swallowed, hardly daring to believe what she was hearing.

"Are you feeling the same as me?" He brushed aside her hair. "Tell me now, if you are not, and I will take my hand from your arm. Tell me quickly," he whispered as he dipped his head to hers, "so that I make no mistakes."

She sucked in a sudden breath, as his closeness deluged her senses with his smell, his presence, his eyes, his lips, so close to hers. But she didn't want to make a mistake either. "I don't know what you're feeling so how can I say if it's the same?"

He lifted a strand of her hair, his eyes tracing the twist of it between his fingertips. "So cautious. Well, I shan't be. Each hour of each day I've been with you, you've revealed yourself to me, little by little, as if your brightness would be too overwhelming to be revealed all at once. I've never known such hunger to be with someone. The more I know about you, the more I want to know. I think about you at night, before I sleep, and I think about you once more when I awake. And then there are my dreams. Cara, I want to make love to you, but only if you are sure, because I cannot promise anything beyond now. My relationships are, by necessity, brief and casual. I want my children to be raised correctly, with no whisper of scandal. There can be no future other than what we have in the present."

She nodded, her throat too constricted to say anything. Her breath hitched in her lungs and her eyes watered with emotion. He frowned as if not sure of her meaning. She nodded again more vigorously. "Yes," she managed to whisper. "Yes, I want you. And just for now works for me, too."

She could have it all. *Him. Now.* And then, tell him the truth later when he no longer wanted her.

He took her hand and they retraced their steps back to the palace. Except, this time, they made their way to Tariq's suite.

CHAPTER 8

Outside his door, he stopped, pulled her close to him and searched her face. "Are you sure about this?"

She nodded. She couldn't do anything else but agree. The way he looked at her, the way his hands slid into her hair, his thumbs brushing along her cheeks so tenderly, despite the need she could feel in his body. He held her as if he cherished her beyond everything, and in that moment she *felt* as if she was the most special woman in the world. If she had any more thoughts or doubts, *that* feeling stemmed them. It might not be logical, it might be stupid, but she could no more fight it than stop a wave from breaking.

She kissed his palm, enjoyed the thrill of her lips next to his skin for one long moment, before looking up at him. A frown deepened with each passing second she hadn't answered. She felt a small leap of joy inside her at his insecurity. "Yes, very sure."

He closed his eyes briefly before he gripped her hand and pulled her into the room. The room was as impressive as the rest of the palace, with a seating area arranged near open doors that led into a private garden. But her eyes didn't linger on the fineries of the room; her attention was drawn to the adjoining room where the flick of a curtain moving in the gentle breeze, caught her eye. The curtain fell from the upright of a tester bed.

Tariq suddenly seemed unsure. In some ways, if he'd been very sure of himself, she thought she probably would have fled. But looking at him, so strangely uncertain, she melted just a little more.

"Would you like a drink?" He stood back from her. As if trying to give them space to think. But thinking was the last thing she wanted to do.

She shook her head. "No." She walked up to him and stood too close, noting the sudden flare of his nostrils and the darkening of his eyes as confusion gave way to lust once more. She lifted her hands and tentatively placed them on his bare chest, her palms caressing his muscles, skimming against the wiry hairs. She watched her hands as they brazenly moved over his skin and then looked up at him suddenly. His eyes were dark and the chest under her fingers was rising and falling with increasing need. "No, I don't want a drink. It's *you* I want."

He lowered his head, his eyes narrowing as they focused intently on her. His hands slid around her back and brought her tight against him. She could feel every hard inch of his body—from his chest, her breasts against his tightly muscled stomach and lower. It was as if he was showing her what was going to happen, giving her yet another chance to escape. She could hardly believe his humility, his reluctance to take anything from someone. He, a King, who could have anything at any time, refused to *take* without permission.

She wriggled closer still and pressed against him, showing him by her movement that *this* was what she wanted. She fanned her fingers around his back, wanting to feel as much of his skin as she could. But *still* he made no move to kiss her. She tilted her head up, lifted her lips closer to his, as her hands slid lower down his back, her fingers skimming the curve of his behind. A tremor ran through his body which stopped only when he pressed his lips to hers.

His kiss was gentle at first, his lips moving over hers like a caress, persuading, exploring and then finally, demanding. He wanted her and she wanted nothing more than to give herself to him. All her world was focused on that one point of connection. And, when he parted his lips, she slipped her tongue into his mouth and she felt his groan move up his body and pass into her mouth, creating a ripple of sensation, deep inside.

Her body moved with an unselfconsciousness she'd never before experienced. Everything she did, from her hands snaking up his back, around his neck and pushing through his hair, to her hips that wriggled against his erection, was rewarded with an immediate response from him. She felt her power for the first time and reveled in it.

When they pulled away, they were both panting.

"Tariq, I need you. *Now*."

He took her hand and pulled her into the bedroom. "You shall have me, *habibi*, but I will have you first. Come." Slowly he undid the tie that held her dress together and slipped it off her shoulders. She stood only in panties and bra. She shivered. "Are you cold?"

She shook her head. "No, I'm hot."

He nodded, his eyes narrowed as he looked over her body. Cara didn't need to look down to know that her nipples were tight and visible through her sheer bra. And it struck her with a distant sense of surprise that she didn't feel awkward standing in front of him nearly naked. She knew that, without clothes, her body came into its own. The curves of her small frame, so easily swamped by clothes, were now visible for him to see.

"You are so beautiful."

She closed her eyes under the powerful sensation his words created. For the first time in her life she *felt* beautiful. For the first time in her life, she felt *alive*.

His appreciation made her feel bold and she opened her eyes and met his gaze as she unfastened her bra and let it slide off her arms. He dropped his gaze to her breasts and she gasped lightly as he brushed her nipples with his fingertips. Then he withdrew his hands and looked up into her eyes. Whatever he saw there sparked a change in him.

He slid both hands under her bottom and picked her up, kissing her as he did so. She wrapped her legs around him, feeling the heaviness of his erection pressing against the wet crotch of her panties. With his tongue invading her mouth, she moved against him again and again, brazenly showing him what she wanted. She'd never done that before, never wanted anyone so much.

He walked her over to the bed and laid her gently down. He pulled down her panties and ran his hands up behind her calves, her knees and her thighs, before he spread them wide and knelt before her.

She cried out and gripped his shoulders as he kissed her intimately. With his tongue, he traced around the damp place where she wanted him to be.

"You are so wet, *habibi*. For *me*."

She clutched his head, wanting him to lift his mouth and kiss her. But as his mouth took control of her once more, his tongue first flicking to the point where all her sensations coalesced, she felt the first rippling sensations which had always before proved elusive. Her hands now held him in place.

Never before had anyone done this to her, and never before had she experienced such sensations. The coiling and whirling tensions built inside her and she gasped, again and again, her fingers digging into his scalp, her body shifting slightly to give him better access. And he made the most of it.

The sensations deepened and she opened her eyes wide and cried out as ecstasy flooded her. With her body still reeling from the blast of sensation, she released her grip on his head and he raised his eyes to hers, a satisfied expression in his eyes.

Slowly he moved up her body, kissing her stomach and then each breast before he stood up. He pulled off his shorts and she couldn't take her eyes off him. His erection was thick and long and she actually felt her mouth salivate when she saw it, she wanted him so much. She sat up on the bed, and tucked her legs under her as he came closer. She wanted to reciprocate, wanted to give to him what he'd just given to her.

The first tentative lick was rewarded with a groan, a tightening of his hands on her shoulders as he threw his head back and she moved her tongue along his length, following the exploration of her fingers, aware of the tension in every muscle of his body.

She pulled away, astounded at her boldness. She'd never done such a thing before. Her husband had been the only person she'd gone to bed with, and sex had always been short, to the point, and not entirely satisfactory for her. That a world of sensation existed, such as Tariq was showing her, was a revelation. And she wanted to know how far that world extended.

Slowly and surely she slid her mouth over his length, as far as she could go. His hips flexed as he slipped in a little deeper before he pulled himself away.

"*Habibi*, I want to see you."

He took her hand and she stood up to face him.

"Here I am," she whispered. "What is it you want to see?"

"Your face, when I make love to you. I've seen it change

with each passing emotion—when you're angry, when you're stubborn, when you're confused, thoughtful, all these things are revealed in your expression. I've never seen a face so expressive. I would watch it now, see what it tells me as I enter you."

She shuddered with suppressed desire and nodded. He leaned over and took a condom from the bedside cabinet. He smiled. "A thoughtful host."

"Or hostess," said Cara, thinking of Anna's perceptiveness. But the thought broke the spell their bodies had cast. He approached her, rolling on the condom as she wriggled back onto the bed.

He noticed her reaction instantly. "What is it?" He reached out his hand to her.

He'd stop, even now, if she wanted him to. She knew that. She trusted him. Nothing but the truth would do. "It's just that I can't believe I'm here, with you. I never do things like this."

His face relaxed. "I know you don't." She wove her fingers through his and he curled his hand over hers. "And if you don't wish to continue, you must tell me now."

She brought their joined fists to her lips and kissed him, closing her eyes as the demands of her body clamored for attention. She could no more deny them than refuse water when she was thirsty. She nodded and opened her eyes. "I want you."

It was all she needed to say. He swept her into his arms and held her hard against his body, moving with a deliberation and urgency that she knew would not diminish. There was no going back now. And she didn't want to.

She wrapped her legs up around his hips and, as he held her close, his gaze never leaving hers, he thrust into her strongly and slid home. She gasped as he filled her so completely, finding her center and her body melted around him.

He moved away slightly as he pulled out of her, eyes narrowed, watching her reactions as he thrust back into her. She cried out at the surge of sensation. Then he slowly withdrew again. She opened her mouth to speak but he touched her lips with his finger and shook his head, before thrusting into her. This time the sensations were even more intense, bringing her to the brink of orgasm.

He sensed she was close and withdrew and thrust again, repeatedly, each thrust taking her closer to where she wanted to be. A little further, a little more, like climbing a ladder, each thrust taking her to another level, one more rung, sending her closer to the top, to a place where she could be free; to the place where she could jump off into an oblivion that was also a freedom, which only he could give her. He held the key to her bliss with his body and he knew it. She felt it in every fiber of her being. She was his to command. And once again he withdrew and thrust and she came in an explosion of light.

His intense gaze only lessened when she looked up at him, with eyes wide, shocked at the sensations that had blasted through her, echoes of which still lingered. Only then did a faint satisfied smile settle on his lips, lips which he placed on hers as he continued to thrust into her. She moved against his hard body, aware of the shortening of his breath against her mouth as she shifted her hips, her hands and flexed the muscles within her, trying to shake his control. She succeeded—in breaking both her control and his, simultaneously, loudly.

He rolled to his side—still holding her, cradling her in his arms—and kissed her hair. "Cara, that was amazing. *You* are amazing."

She stroked up the side of his hip as she regained her

breath, tracing the strong muscles over his stomach, his chest and up to his shoulders. She stopped there. There was something about his shoulders, so broad, so strong. They were the shoulders of a king, capable of carrying a load heavier than most people could bear. She thought she'd never forget this moment. She could see the depth of his personality in everything about him—from the way he held her, to the expression in his eyes. No sunlight penetrated the shady rooms and yet she felt as if she could see more clearly than she ever had before. He'd awakened her from a self-imposed sleep where she'd been immune to everything—protected yes, but from both the bad and the good. He'd broken down the barriers she'd erected between her and the world, and given her life back.

"And so are you," she murmured. She felt herself choking up. She lowered her lids, focusing on her fingers as they explored his shoulders and chest, hoping he wouldn't notice.

"Cara?" He moved his head lower to look into her eyes but she turned away. He lifted her face with his hand. "What's wrong?" His finger traced one of the tears down her cheek. "Did I hurt you?"

He looked so concerned, that she couldn't help but smile through her tears. She shook her head and took in a gasping breath, trying to wipe the tears away. "No. It's just…"

"What? You don't regret it?"

"No, of course not. How could I? It was wonderful. More wonderful than I knew possible."

"You've never felt that way before? You've never…"

She understood his unfinished question. She shook her head. "Never before."

He pulled her to him. "Then you must have chosen your boyfriends badly."

"Boy*friend*," she repeated wanting to tell him. Now. "Only one. He became—"

"Hush." He placed his finger against her lips. "I don't wish to hear further of a man who couldn't satisfy his woman. You are with me now." He nudged himself inside her again and a wave of pleasure swept her body as she immediately responded to the stimulation. "I will pleasure you again and again until you tell me to stop."

"And what," she said, sliding around until she was on top of him, "if I pleasure you? If I take control?"

He lay back, his hands on her hips as she moved up and down on top of him. "You do as you wish, *habibi*."

And she did.

TARIQ DIDN'T KNOW how long he'd stood by the open window, alternately watching Cara sleep under the light of a flickering candle, and watching the pre-dawn light strengthen over the mountains.

A day of lovemaking had drifted into night, which was slowly turning into dawn. Cara's eyelids flickered open and he could see brief confusion turn to recognition.

"Tariq!" The happy surprise in her tone and smile turned into a brief frown. His own misgivings must be evident on his face. She rose and his thoughts fled while he drank in the perfect curves of her body. She slipped the orange dress she'd worn the previous night over her nakedness and took his hand.

"You should wear colors like that more often—orange, red, yellow—the colors of the sun. You hide yourself too much."

"I prefer it that way. But why have you risen so early? What is it?"

He extended his hand to hers. "I've been dreading the coming of the sun, *habibi*." He pulled her in close, inhaling her perfume, immediately filled with want. "For when the sun comes, we will have to leave here and continue our lives."

She nodded. "I know. And that's okay. You didn't offer anything more, and I have my own life to live." She bit her lip and smiled a sudden, slight smile, as if she were hiding something. There was so much he didn't know about her; so much he had no right to ask. "It's the way it has to be."

"It is." He heard the rise in intonation which betrayed his doubt. "However, the sun hasn't yet risen," he continued, carefully ensuring he hid any trace of his real feelings. There was no place in his life for those. "Come, *habibi*, let's walk outside."

He held the gauzy curtain aside and she passed through the door, her body clearly visible through the fine stuff of her dress, her nipples peaking as she stepped out in the fresh, early morning air.

The sun had yet to rise over the mountains and the sky was filled with grey clouds, streaked with gold intensifying into orange and red with each passing minute.

"Rain clouds? It's not allowed to rain here. Doesn't it know it's a desert?" She trembled.

"You're shivering," he murmured before he kissed her hair, now wet with the first drops of rain. "And it's raining. Do you wish to return inside? I recall you don't like the rain."

"It's true, I don't."

"Why? It's life-giving. It's beautiful. Look."

Even as they spoke the dark clouds amassed and the grey clouds turned a dark purple from which heavy sheets of rain began to fall, darkening the ground instantly and soaking them.

"It's different rain, here," she murmured. She leaned her head on his shoulder. "It was cold, torrential rain the week my father died."

"Tell me."

"It started with a thunder storm and the electricity was cut for miles around. The doctors said afterwards the lack of dialysis wouldn't have made any difference. He was dying. It rained constantly for weeks after he died. It was still raining when my mother died."

"Hence your dislike for the rain."

"I *didn't* like it," she added with emphasis. "But it's different now." She looked up at him with eyes so trusting that it almost broke his heart. She reached up on her tip toes and kissed him, before rocking back onto her heels again. "It seems that many things have changed this morning."

He didn't ask what had changed. Because it made what he was doing to her even harder for him to bear. He needed to move. He tugged her hand and they walked under the towering palms, whose massive leaves twitched under the onslaught of the rain. It joined the water that flowed from the natural springs in the mountains along the runnels and rills that took it down further to water the gardens and fountains of other secret gardens that lay within the confines of the rambling palace.

They were soon soaked to the skin, which Tariq couldn't regret. Cara's dress clung to her, revealing her breasts and stomach and body in tantalizing detail. He halted her and kissed her, wanting her there and then. He began to lift her dress but she laughed and stopped him, kissing him open mouthed and sensually on the lips before stepping away.

"You look like some wild unearthly woman formed from the water to tempt me, to drive me out of my wits."

She flung her head back allowing the rain onto her face. He kissed her neck. "I feel wild."

"What else do you feel?" he murmured as his lips sought out the warmth of her neck.

"It's as if I can smell every scent of the flowers, of the dry earth soaked by the rain, of you…" She turned her face to kiss him. "It's as if I've awoken from a long, dreamless sleep, rested and alive for the first time in my life."

There was such a complex look of innocence, trust and sensuality in her expression that Tariq froze. What the hell was he doing?

At that moment, as quickly as it arrived, the rain stopped and the dark cloud passed over, leaving a watery sun rising over the mountain ridge and warm air in its wake. They were both silent as they watched the colors shift and re-form into all the colors of the rainbow.

"Cara, you know there can be no future between us. I'm a solitary man, except for my children. After my marriage ended with Laiha's death, I vowed never to marry again."

"And I don't want anything more than we have now, Tariq. I'll be leaving for England and then Italy next week and beginning a new life, away from here."

He exhaled his breath in a sigh. Of course. "A new life…" he repeated. "And what is it you intend to do there, Cara?"

She leaned back against his chest, as his arms wrapped around her. "Translate. I've a few jobs lined up. They're not lucrative, but will provide enough to live on."

"If you ever need—"

She swung around in his embrace, her face full of hurt. "You think I want your money?"

Tariq looked down at her delicate face so full of beauty and life. He'd never wanted anyone as much in his life. He felt like a dying man reaching out for the sun, reaching out for life, as his fingers traced her cheek, her jaw, her eyes, bright in the early morning sunshine. "No, *habibi*, no I don't. I just want you safe, that's all."

"And I will be."

He nodded, sadly. "The sun is up; we should be away. The Aurus people won't be arriving in the city until tomorrow. If you're not busy perhaps you will accompany me back to the palace?"

"Sure. That'll be lovely."

He hesitated. "Then tomorrow. We'll be meeting with them in the afternoon. You'll be there for that last meeting?"

He saw the surprise in her eyes that she wasn't required before that time. But surprise was preferable to the dismay which would follow. He had a day to steel himself for that. He hadn't expected to feel so bad about using her for his own ends. He hadn't imagined he could experience such feelings for a woman again after the years of bitterness following his wife's betrayal.

His focus on her swam a little and then he bowed his head to hers and kissed her, his heart pounding. He was right. Life was here, in her. And he was thirsty for it, no matter what the day brought for them both.

He trailed his hand down her arm and wrapped her small hand in his, tight. In that moment he thought he'd never let her go, and drew back so he could see her better. He could feel the thudding of her pulse against his finger and see her darkening eyes, her lips parted and soft, and for the first time in his life he felt nothing of what was going on around him. He forgot the world, forgot himself and his needs, forgot his country. He was a man, *here, now*, with the only woman he wanted. He couldn't say any of these things to her, but he could show her.

She must have sensed something of his thoughts because when he pulled her by the hand back to the bedroom she came willingly as if realizing his intention. And, as soon as they entered the bedroom, she turned to him and, with fumbling fingers, undid his clothes, as he pulled her wet dress, the color of a sunrise delayed by the rain, from her body.

As her mouth found his and she kissed him hungrily, all

thought of their return to the city faded. What had started off so easily, to take her away from the Aurus execs, to stop her from communicating her doubts as to the real state of the riches that lay under Jabal al Kanz, had turned into something quite different. Something he knew he would regret when she turned her green eyes to him, full of anger and bitterness, when she learned just how much he'd used her.

CHAPTER 9

The sun was high and, just as Tariq had predicted, they were in the air, flying back to the city palace. Cara turned and looked down at the Palace of Qawaran with regret. She was leaving a different person and had made friends there who she'd never see again.

He squeezed her hand and she turned to face him. He brought her hand to his lips and kissed it. "Thank you for coming with me to Qawaran."

She grinned. "I don't remember being exactly asked. More of a command, if I remember right." She grinned and squinted her eyes, the sky bright even with sunglasses.

He shrugged. "I'm sorry. I'm used to giving orders. Besides, I *am* paying you."

She frowned but a smile twitched on his lips. Any anger at his comment dissipated as her eyes dwelt on lips that expressed a humor that he kept well hidden. Seeing him relaxed and in a teasing mood warmed her through and through. "Um..." She swallowed, trying to restrain herself from undoing her belt and kissing those lips. "For what though?" she asked, quite happy to tease back. She raised an eyebrow as he glanced at her. "Because it's not like I did any translation."

"Ah, an underhand ploy to enjoy your company." He looked suddenly concerned. "I planned nothing else, you understand."

She knew he hadn't planned to seduce her. It had grown out of nowhere and he'd been considerate of her needs, too willing to back away if she wanted him to, to have planned it all. She knew him better now and knew that wasn't his style. He was a man of integrity and honor, a man who wouldn't use a woman that way.

"Yes, I know."

"So you have no regrets?"

She shook her head, her eyes ranging over his face, a face she'd come to know and... have feelings for. "No. I don't regret a thing." Later she might, but not now.

He looked at her with a super sexy smile that made her gut flutter and tighten with desire. "Not even when I insisted we stand out in the rain?"

"Well, maybe a little then."

"Not even when you chewed the wild pistachio nut?

"Most definitely then. You didn't tell me it tasted like turpentine."

"An oversight. But no regrets over anything else?"

She knew he meant their night together but she'd do a little teasing of her own.

"No, how could I regret meeting such great people? Anna and Lucy were lovely. In a different life I think we could even have been friends."

His expression changed then. "'A different life'...Fate, Cara, has given us only one life."

She turned to the view. "I know." She had to tell him something of what the night had meant to her. "Tariq. We'll be landing soon and things will be different. I know that.

And it's fine with me. But I want you to know that last night meant a lot to me. I can't explain how, it's too complicated, too personal. But it made me *feel* in a way I haven't in a very long time. And I want to thank you for that."

Was the sun reflecting off the city towers they were so rapidly approaching, so bright that it made him turn from her and narrow his eyes? Was he so unwilling to answer that he had to bring his lips together in a tight line to stop himself from speaking? He shook his head jerkily in an ambiguous movement. "I can't…"

"It's okay."

He nodded and cleared his throat. "We'll be landing soon, make sure your seat belt is secure."

As responses went to thanking someone for sex, it wasn't the best, Cara felt, as she obediently tightened her belt. But she wasn't as offended as she felt she probably should have been. She watched him as he checked his controls, ready for landing. He was a complex man, a man with the weight of a country and a bad marriage on his shoulders. He was a man who wasn't free to speak of his feelings, or even to indulge in them. The country's gain… and her loss.

THERE WAS a car waiting for them on the airport tarmac, shimmering in the mid-day sun. Tariq exchanged brief greetings with his driver who passed him a file of papers.

As Cara slipped into the seat beside him, Tariq looked down at the papers and phone briefly, before pushing them to one side.

Instead he discreetly held her hand and they talked of inconsequential things as they drove back to the palace.

The car pulled up around the rear entrance and Tariq waved away the driver and held the car door open for Cara. They walked to the private entrance of the palace and Tariq raised his hand to push open the door but stopped and turned to her, pausing in the privacy of the entrance way.

"Cara…"

"What is it?"

He trailed his finger down her cheek before curling it around and lifting her chin until their faces were close.

"Do you trust me?"

She half-laughed. "Of course." Then she frowned as his eyes didn't leave her face and she felt the seriousness and intensity of his gaze. Suddenly she felt uncomfortable. "Is there any reason why I shouldn't?"

He didn't answer immediately and a shiver tracked down her spine.

"We know so little of each other." His voice was hoarser than before, almost tentative.

She reached up and touched his face, needing to feel the reality of his skin against hers once more, wanting to show him that they *did* know each other, despite what the tracking of days showed. She shouldn't trust him, she knew she shouldn't. She'd vowed never to trust another man after her husband. After all she hardly knew him. But as she looked up into his eyes, she knew she did.

"I trust you, Tariq. I know what it feels like to have you close to me, to breathe your breath, to look into your eyes when you think no one needs anything from you and when you're desperate for something that still you don't take." She nodded slowly. "Yes, I trust you."

He closed his eyes and turned her hand, kissing the palm. In that moment she knew she trusted him more than she'd ever trusted anyone in her life.

His mood changed in an instant—suddenly becoming determined, agitated even. He grabbed both her hands in his and brought them up between them both, grasping them as if in prayer. "You don't know me, despite last night, but I need you to have faith in me, to trust in me."

A shadow fell between them and her frown deepened. "What is it? You can tell me."

"I am sheikh, Cara. Leader of my people. *King*. I have responsibilities that are far greater than those of an ordinary man." He pressed a kiss to her still-clenched hands. "Know this. And don't forget it." His grip tightened. "Tell me you won't forget."

She tried to shift her hands from his grip but she couldn't. Her heart thudded heavily as she drew in shorter, ragged breaths. "Let me go, Tariq."

"Tell me," he repeated.

"You are a man to me, first and foremost." She swallowed. "But you are also King, sheikh of your people. Even if I could forget that, I'll be reminded as soon as we walk through that door."

He frowned and searched her face and then nodded as if satisfied and looked down at his hands holding hers, too tightly, and sprung them apart. She rubbed her hands together.

"I'm sorry. Have I hurt you?"

She shook her head. He hadn't even noticed how tight he'd been gripping her, he was so consumed with the notion of her trusting him. "No." Not yet he hadn't. But she knew he would. Because no matter how much she trusted him, she'd feel the pain when she left.

"Good. No matter what is said today, remember my words."

She was about to ask him why, but he pre-empted her question with a kiss that robbed her of any thoughts. He brought her hard against him as the kiss deepened. Just as her legs threatened to give way beneath her, he pulled away as abruptly. She thought she saw him shake his head before turning and pushing open the door.

Inside the private entrance foyer, they stopped while Tariq spoke to an assistant. She looked all around at the luxury—all gleaming surfaces, white on gold—and shivered. The stark contrast to Qusayr Zarqa was great. The chandelier sparkled under both the lights of the electric bulbs and the refracted light from the sun. It was too much, too sparkly and… too cold, she realized. It was a beautiful space but was full of furniture that somehow didn't seem to belong, either to Ma'in or to Tariq. Despite the heat, the palace—even the private quarters—felt impersonal and cold.

The assistant bowed and left and Tariq joined her. "What is it? Are you all right?"

"Yes," she shrugged, "it's just…" She shivered once more. "Someone walking over my grave."

It was his turn to frown. "Don't say that."

"It's just an expression, it means—"

"Expression or not, don't say it. Now come. I want you to meet my family."

As they entered a room two children rose from formal chairs. The boy, about eight years old, was still under the restraining hold of his serious-looking elder sister, who appeared to be about twelve. The boy seemed nervous as they approached Tariq and Cara.

"Father," the girl greeted him formally, her impassive face breaking into a brief warm smile that utterly transformed her looks. Her father's daughter, Cara thought. "You've returned earlier than we imagined." She turned with a cool glance to Cara. Tariq followed her gaze.

"Cara, let me introduce you to my son, Gadiel—who will be nine tomorrow—and my daughter, Saarah."

"Pleased to meet you." The idea of curtseying briefly ran through Cara's mind but it seemed silly with children so young. She stepped forward with her hand extended in greeting.

Saarah looked at her hand with disapproval and then looked up at her father.

"This is Cara Devlin…" His pause made Cara wonder how she was going to be introduced. "A translator."

"Then what is she doing here, father?"

"Mind you manners, Saarah!" Tariq said quietly, the warning in his voice not going unnoticed judging by the flush of heat on the young girl's face. "Miss Devlin is my guest, and therefore she is *yours*, also."

Saarah turned to Cara, the slight smile hardly there, but it seemed to satisfy her father. "Miss Devlin. Welcome. Would you care for refreshment?"

Cara had never met such a collected twelve-year-old. Nor such an arrogant one. "Yes, please. That would be lovely."

"Where's Eshal?" asked Tariq.

"With her nanny. They'll be joining us shortly."

They all walked into a reception room, every bit as grandly furnished as the hall, and every bit as austere.

While Saarah arranged the refreshments, Gadiel showed Tariq and Cara the *Harry Potter* books he was reading and Cara promised to bring him some books by another author she thought he'd like. Once the quiet boy had discovered Cara loved books, just as he did, he didn't stop talking, even inviting her to his birthday party the following day. It was only when Saarah took her seat opposite Cara, her level gaze fixed on her, that the boy returned to silence once more.

While Tariq took Gadiel off to show him something, Cara and Saarah sat in silence. Cara was relieved when the door opened and a little girl of around two was brought in, wriggling in the arms of her nurse.

"And this," Tariq said with a grin, returning into the room at the same time, "is Eshal."

The family were distracted while Eshal noisily insisted on being put down, whereupon she made straight for Cara, grabbing her dress in a fist as she looked up at Cara with a disarming smile. Cara smiled warily as she tried to free her dress from the toddler's firm grip. She'd never spent time with children, and wasn't comfortable with them. Piers hadn't wanted children and so she'd always avoided them, not wanting to want something she could never have.

She tried to step away but Eshal held on with a determination she was beginning to see was a family trait. She moved again and her dress tugged sharply out from Eshal's grip, taking her by surprise, and knocking her off balance. As if in slow motion, Cara could see the little girl's head plummeting toward the sharp edge of a coffee table. Instinctively, Cara scooped her up and out of danger before she could hurt herself.

Eshal took the opportunity of wrapping her plump arms around Cara with the triumphant smile of someone who'd got what she wanted. Not knowing the barriers that her elder sister knew all too well, Eshal brought up her hand and stroked Cara's cheek. "Pretty," she said. In that instant Cara knew she'd fallen for the child. Eshal could have said 'ugly' and she'd still have fallen for her. Eshal lifted her fingers to Cara's ear-rings and began playing with them. It was the silence that made her look around.

Everyone was looking at her oddly: Saarah with shocked eyes, Gadiel with an open mouth and Tariq, Tariq was looking at her with a heated gaze that was as all-encompassing as Eshal's arms that were now wrapped around Cara's body, like they were never going to let go.

"Eshal!" Saarah said, when she'd recovered. "Get down at once."

"She's okay," said Cara, grinning down at Eshal.

"It's certainly not okay," replied Saarah. "You are a guest and she is being too familiar."

"No need to stand on ceremony with me, Saarah."

Cara exchanged looks with Tariq. Tariq suddenly became aware of his daughter's remarks and turned to her. "If… Miss Devlin is happy to have Eshal in her arms, then I don't see the problem, do you?"

Saarah bit her lip, eyes blazing. "Please excuse me, father. I have to study."

He was about to remonstrate but Cara shot him another look and, to her surprise, he just nodded. "Go then, I will see you at dinner."

"We are expected at Jadda's tonight for dinner, father. Remember, we had not expected you until tomorrow."

"Of course. Tomorrow night, then, Saarah."

"Come, Gadiel," Saarah called to the boy who reluctantly trailed after her.

"And let Nurse know that Eshal's ready for her, too." Tariq called after her.

Cara was left holding Eshal.

"You're a natural with her. She's quiet with you." He came and caressed Eshal's soft thick hair. "She's a handful, always has been. Very demanding."

Eshal looked up at her father quizzically. Cara smiled at the child's mobile features, shifting and changing, mercurial. The child twisted in Cara's arms and shot her hands out to her father, who took her into his arms. She immediately placed her cheek against her chest and began sucking her thumb.

"Demanding, like that, demanding?"

At that moment the nurse entered the room and his assistant bowed at the door. Tariq turned to Cara. She knew he needed to go.

"I'll go now, back to my apartment. I'll return tomorrow for the last meeting... if you need me?"

"I need you." He sighed. "I'll have someone bring a car round for you. Aarif will make sure you get home safely." He stepped away from her. "Tomorrow then." He turned and walked away.

Cara barely heard Aarif's polite conversation as they walked through the palace. All she could think of was that she was falling for a man who would despise her when he learned of her connection with the thief who'd attempted to rob Ma'in of its most precious artifacts. It was the worst crime possible from Tariq's perspective—stealing another's identity, another's culture, his heritage. And she was still married to the man who'd carried it out.

Yes, she might be falling for Tariq, had already fallen for his youngest child, but there was no future. As soon as she had the money, she had to do as she'd planned, buy herself tickets to London and then on to Italy. And return the statue to Tariq. In that order. There was no way she'd be able to see Tariq after that. She'd leave this world of disappointed dreams and heartaches behind. Including him.

~

It was late in the day when the intercom on her central city apartment buzzed. Cara sighed but didn't look away from her view over the city. No doubt it was a mistake. No one knew she was here. Whoever it was would go away soon.

She let her head fall back once more against the only chair in the apartment—everything else had been packed away. The evening light streamed into the empty room and onto the small priceless statue. She was tired and numb. She'd spent the day packing and making arrangements for the return of the statue, after discovering the fee for her work with Tariq had been paid in full. Just a few more things to do—a statue in a courier parcel and a letter for Tariq.

The buzzer sounded again and this time it penetrated her reverie. It couldn't be anyone she knew. She'd cut herself off from her old world, of her husband's old world, she reminded herself. After the scandal she no longer saw any of her father's friends from the university. There was no one who knew she lived here, not even the agency who found her her jobs. She sighed and walked over to the intercom and pressed the button.

"Cara. It's me."

She let go in shock, then pressed it again. "Tariq? I mean, Your—"

"I think we're beyond that, don't you?" She could hear the smile in his words. She pressed her forehead against the wall above the intercom and licked her lips.

"Yes, I guess we are."

There was a long pause. "Cara, will you come with me now? Dinner maybe?"

"I've eaten." She stalled.

"So have I. It's an excuse. I want your company."

"I thought—"

"I know what you thought. But we have one more evening before our business concludes, before our lives go their different ways. And I wanted to spend it with you. Will you come?"

She should say no. There were a thousand reasons to say 'no'. They were from different worlds and, not least, she was deceiving him every moment she was with him. "Yes," she heard herself answer. She winced but didn't change her mind. "Yes, give me a minute. I'll be right down." She glanced at the small statue sitting on the window sill. Piers had left it in the apartment claiming it was worthless and why wouldn't she believe him? He'd locked away everything else of value.

But he'd been clever with this, probably the most valuable of them all. No doubt he'd planned a brief reconciliation to redeem it.

She felt a rush of guilt at what she was hiding from Tariq. She trailed her fingers over its smooth curves. She desperately wanted to walk out of the apartment with the statue and hand it to him. Then and there. Get it over with. But she knew what would happen next. The look of disgust he'd throw at her would be inevitable when he finally understood her connection to the thief. And she'd have to face that later. Not now. Not before she'd left Ma'in because she knew what the prison term for theft was. No. It would have to wait. Just a few more days and then it would be back where it belonged and she'd be gone.

But, she thought as she grabbed her abaya and bag, we have tonight. She cast one quick glance at the statue and left the room.

To her surprise Tariq was alone, dressed in European clothes.

"You look beautiful," he said as he opened the door of his car—no driver tonight, she noticed—and she jumped in and they roared off up the broad avenue away from the palace.

"I thought we were going to the palace?"

"No." His eyes were fixed on the road ahead.

"Then where are we going?"

"To Qusayr Zarqa. Just for tonight."

He shot her a quick intense look and she turned away as the heat flared between them. She knew what he wanted because she wanted exactly the same.

He ground his teeth, as if he was desperate for control. "Talk to me."

She drew in a deep breath of air, trying to focus on anything but the demands of her body. "About what?"

"Anything! Anything to take my mind of the fact that I want to stop this car and make love to you."

"Right," she whispered faintly, stretching forward to turn up the air conditioning. "Okay"—she swallowed—"your children are lovely."

It seemed to work. He sighed deeply and nodded. "You made quite an impression on Eshal. When I saw her later she kept pointing to where you'd been and chattering about something incomprehensible. I had to explain you'd gone."

"And your son is a darling."

"Yes, he's easier than either of the girls. He's too quiet though. Loves reading and only comes hunting with me on sufferance. But he'll make a good King. And as for Saarah, I apologize. Since my wife died, she appears to consider she's in control of the family. She's become arrogant."

"She's only twelve, Tariq. All girls are difficult at that age."

"Even you?" He smiled. "I can imagine you at that age. Quietly getting what you want without anyone noticing."

She grinned, unable to contradict him. "Actually you're right. I usually did get what I want. Usually, not always. Not later."

She stopped herself, but not before he cast her an inquisitive look. "Go on."

"No, tell me about you." She turned in her seat and placed her hand lightly on his thigh.

"I can't even think with your hand on my leg." At that moment the desert palace appeared on the horizon in the dying light. She went to move her hand and he clasped it back into place, his hand crushing hers. "Leave it there. I don't want to think."

As they approached, the gates were swung open and he drove inside the courtyard and parked. They were met by the housekeeper and a skeleton staff who were all rapidly dismissed.

"Why is it so dark?" she asked as they entered the vast hall, stretching two stories high, wall sconces alight with naked flames which stuttered under the influence of the open door, casting moving shadows in the empty hall.

"I prefer it this way."

She shivered. For one moment she felt as if she'd stepped back into a medieval world where their passion fitted. Raw, unadulterated passion in a raw, primitive world. She caught her breath as the notion refused to leave.

"Come." He tugged her hand and she had to run to keep up with him, run as they moved through the vast hall, up the steps, and along the winding corridors towards a wing of the palace where she'd not been before.

He opened the door to his room, a corner suite that had windows on all three sides, the fourth side extending beyond walls which had been removed to create a master suite of massive proportions. He moved from the sitting room, past a library through to the bedroom. There he turned to her and kissed her, long and hard. She responded with a passion equal to his own.

He pulled her tight against him and she could feel his arousal. She slipped her hands under his white shirt and around his back, needing to feel the heat of his skin under her fingers. It was like touching heated stone—hard, unflinching—as powerful as the rest of him.

He'd lit no lights. The ornate shutters were open to the evening air, the sounds of the desert calling to them from outside. She felt a part of it all, as if she belonged to this wild place.

She lifted her lips to his and he pressed his mouth against hers. She felt his shuddering sigh of desire against her cheek, as his hand rose and raked his fingers through her hair, holding her steady, as if making sure she wouldn't escape. But she wasn't going anywhere. All she was, was a sum total of her senses, and all her senses were concentrated on the slow, exquisite movement of his lips against hers. Her lips melted under his and opened. The tip of his tongue touched hers and she gasped against his mouth. Her whole body was electrified, shot with a desire that was like nothing she'd felt before. It slammed into her with its intensity, turning her instantly wet, as she tilted her hips to touch his body.

He groaned against her mouth and the kiss deepened and grew fierce. With each slide of his tongue against hers, with each caress of his fingers, touching where she needed to be touched, the aching, throbbing need for him intensified.

Breathless they pulled away from each other, pressing their foreheads against each other's. "Cara, I've never wanted anyone as much I want you now."

His obvious desire for her made her bold. "And I want you. Do you want to know how much?"

He nodded and she took his hand and moved it down her body, under her dress, across her stomach and lower. She released his hand and fell against him, weak as he explored her and discovered just how much she wanted him. She pushed herself against him but he pulled away, kissing her. "Not yet, Cara."

She undid his shirt and pressed her fingers against his skin, needing to see the reality of him. Then she kissed him. He smelt divine. She pressed her lips to his skin and this time, she licked him. He was like a food, an addiction she didn't know she had until now. She trailed her tongue down, until it met his trousers. She grunted with frustration as she slid her tongue down as far as she could go and was rewarded with the tip of his hard erection. She licked it and felt a sharp intake of breath under her fingers that were still pressed against his chest. But they didn't stay there. She needed him urgently.

She flicked open the button and pushed his trousers and

shorts aside. She rocked back on her heels as he was revealed—broad, long and powerful. She touched it and he shuddered, the tip glistening under the flickering light of the naked flame. She kneeled up and pushed his trousers down so she could see all of him. She licked the heavy sacs that lay beneath his swollen shaft, looked up at him and, with satisfaction, saw his throat constrict, his eyes dark and full of lust, and trained on her. She felt outrageously powerful and with that, came freedom to *do*, to *be*, exactly who she wanted to be. And now, she wanted to pleasure him.

She lifted her head, her eyes not shifting from his, as she took him in her mouth, watching him inhale sharply and his eyes close. She relished his throbbing length under her lips, relished how he responded to her touch. She wanted him however she could get him. Every part of him. She continued to taste, to lick, to move her mouth over him, instinct taking over from lack of knowledge. For tonight, he was her man and she knew how to give him pleasure.

But before he was brought to the height of pleasure, his hands moved from her hair to clasp her hands which he brought out wide. She withdrew her mouth and he pulled her to standing.

"Much more of that and this will be over before it begins." He smiled and lifted her face to his and kissed her. "You are the most incredible woman..." She stopped his words by kissing him again. He lifted her into his arms and continued to kiss her as he walked over to the bed. He stood her onto her feet gently and undid her dress and let it fall at her feet.

He gazed at her, his fingers touching where his eyes had rested, as he absorbed her breasts, rising rapidly in arousal over the half-cup lacy white bra, before trailing down her sides, making her stomach jump as his fingers caught her unawares, pressing under the elastic of her panties. With one swift movement he'd dragged them down and tossed them aside. Then her bra.

As one they fell onto the bed, rumpling the fine white linen sheets, their naked bodies pressing and writhing against each other's, desperate to give pleasure and be pleasured.

Shadows from the leaping flames caught in the high overhead beams and cast a strange, eerie light on his skin, so dark and so exotic. It was like something dangerous and infinitely desirable. It responded to her every touch, with a movement, a caress, a nip, that sparked her need for more. It was like fire playing with fire in the darkness. Shoots of light, of intensity, followed by a hotter fire, simmering, flickering, refusing to be extinguished, needing more with each breath, each touch.

She moved without thought or design, by instinct only, opening her legs and wrapping them around him. She rolled onto her back and he entered her, slipping into her slowly, inch by inch, allowing her body time to accommodate the heft and length of him. She shifted slightly and he pushed all the way inside her. She lifted her face up to his and he took her offered mouth with a kiss full of passion and need and desperation. She didn't know where this desperation came from. All she knew was that he needed her now and she could fulfil that need… and more.

She pulled him to her with her heels, hardly knowing whether the pressure inside her and against her most sensitive skin, was pain or pleasure because such difference held no meaning. It was all passion and it was all that she wanted.

THE NIGHT WENT by in a haze of love-making and drifting in and out of sleep, always with Tariq with his arms around her.

She awoke to feel her name whispered against her cheek. "Cara." Her whispered name sounded like a caress in his deep voice. She opened her eyes to see his face, close, his eyes, tender. "Cara," he shook his head. "How do you do it?"

She rolled her head against the pillow. "Do what?" she whispered, lifting her hand to smooth back his hair.

He raised himself on one elbow and traced a finger down her throat and around her breast. "How is it that you can reach into me, touch me where no one else can?"

"I do that?"

He nodded. "Yes, you do that. You reach beyond where I can protect myself."

She couldn't believe the words he was saying. She tried to "Why would you want to protect yourself?"

"From the forces that destroyed my father and nearly destroyed me, set one of my brothers on a path of gambling and the other to move far away from here. I was so focused on politics and wealth and state affairs that somehow you crept in under my radar. You're like the air that I breathe, entering me, touching me at my center. Something I barely noticed to begin with until suddenly I realize that I feel you in every part of me." He pressed his forehead against hers and rolled lightly against hers with closed eyes. "Sometimes I have the fancy that if I did not have you, like the air inside my body, that I'd be unable to survive."

She rolled away, conscious now that his defenses might have dropped but there was no way she could let hers do the same thing. She shook her head. "You're wrong. That's the lack of sleep, that's the sex, talking. You'll be back to normal in the morning." She rose and slipped on his gown, belting it as she turned to him, pushing her hair from her face. "I prescribe two strong cups of black coffee and a meeting with uncouth foreigners and you'll be back to normal." She turned from the window and gave him a brief, uncertain grin.

He stood up and gripped her shoulders, his eyes fierce. "Don't be flippant, Cara. Don't try to deflect this with humor.

I mean it. Look at you, haloed against the early light." He brushed his fingers against her hair. "Hair that melts against the desert."

"No," she whispered.

He smoothed a finger over her lower lip. "And your voice, a voice that wraps itself around me and tugs me, draws me to you. You're a witch, a chameleon."

"No, I swear, no, Tariq, this isn't me you're describing. This is someone you want me to be."

He slipped his hands down her arms and held both her hands within his and kissed their joined fists. He sighed. "Cara, how can I convince you that you are as beautiful as I see you, that you are as desirable as I describe? That you eclipse other women as the moon covers the sun. You obliterate their light, and claim the sky. You claim *me*. It's you I'm describing; it's you I want, Cara. I want you in my arms, I want my body in yours, joined. I want to see your pale face flushed with the pleasure I bring you."

His words and touch sent a blast of desire through her body. She pressed herself against his naked body and he pushed aside her gown. He was ready for her, as she jumped up and curled her legs around his hips, pushing herself onto him fully. She went crazy, in a frenzy for him, while he gave her what she wanted, but leaned back his head, watching her, just as he said he would.

CHAPTER 10

Too soon, at first light, they were on their way back to the palace. It was a quiet journey, few words said, his hand covering hers as he drove back through the desert, then through the outskirts of the city, already awake and going about its business.

He pulled up the car to her apartment and kissed her. "Rest now and I'll see you later."

"Don't you want me this morning for the meeting?"

"No, I won't need you until this afternoon. Go, now, rest, and I'll have a car come for you at one." He kissed her one last time and, with a growing sense of dread, she watched the car roar down the beautiful avenue. The days were slipping away. She'd see him one last time and then she'd be gone.

IT WAS JUST before two in the afternoon when Cara returned to the palace. She wore the red dress which Tariq had sent to her apartment. He'd been right. She even felt different wearing such bright colors. She walked into the room she'd been shown and was surprised to find it empty, except for a table laid for lunch. For *two people*. She turned to Aarif who'd escorted her there.

"Is there some mistake? Is the meeting elsewhere?"

"No mistake, Miss Devlin, you're expected here. Please, take a seat. His Royal Highness won't be long."

At that moment Tariq swept into the room, as imposing as ever, his white robes falling around him, making him look even taller and more commanding than before. For a brief moment she wondered whether the last few days and nights had been a dream. He looked impossibly out of her league.

He exchanged a few words with Aarif before dismissing him and then he turned to her and the expression in his eyes changed and the last few days, their connection, became a reality once more. He strode over to her and took both her hands in his.

"You came."

Her smile faded a little as she searched his face. He looked preoccupied, worried even. She'd never seen him look anything other than confident and in control. "Of course I did. Is everything all right?" He averted his gaze briefly as trying to collect his thoughts. She realized with surprise that he looked uncomfortable. "And why would you think I wouldn't come anyway?"

"You haven't seen the news, then? I had delayed its release until I saw you, but there was always the possibility that someone might release something on the internet in their rush to be first."

She frowned and shook her head. "What are you talking about? News? What news? And why would you possibly want to delay something until you saw me?"

"There is no meeting. If you knew your services as a translator weren't required, I wasn't sure you'd come. The business had been completed."

"You've signed the contract?" Her heart dropped. She knew how much this meant to him. "I'm sorry."

"No. Sahmir came through. He's raised enough cash through his contacts to enable us to regain control of our land."

"That's fantastic!"

"I couldn't have done it without you."

She frowned, confused. "What did I do?"

"You gave us enough time to secure the finance by stirring their interest in Jabal al Kanz—the mountain of treasure. The Aurus delegation didn't go to Gold Mine I, as they insist on calling it. They went to visit Jabal al Kanz instead."

"But, I thought you made sure they didn't. Besides, that's restricted land." Cara was confused. "They can't go there without your permission." She looked into his eyes and suddenly felt a sinking, sickening feeling in her stomach. She let go of his hands but he gripped harder, refusing to let them slide away. "And you gave it. You knew about it, before I told you, and you allowed it."

"Yes, of course."

"Then why didn't you accompany them? And why on earth did you take me away with you?"

His eyes ranged over her face, as if trying to make her understand by sheer force of will, rather than by words.

"*Tell* me, Tariq."

"You have to remember, Cara, that my country, my heritage, is everything to me. It always has been and *will* always be. I'll do anything for it. I needed them diverted for a couple of days. Your translation provided the perfect distraction."

He fixed her with an intense gaze and a shiver ran down her spine. Her legs suddenly felt weak and she leaned back against the wall. She swallowed before asking the question she had to ask. "You had no intention of allowing our paths to cross again, did you? You knew I had my doubts as to the correct translation, so you decided I needed to be kept away. Hence the sudden invitation to join you in Qawaran. And this morning. 'Rest', you said. It was all a pretense, wasn't it? You, me. It wasn't just them you tricked, but me, too."

Anger flashed into his eyes. "As they tricked my father with their promises of 'civilization'. They murdered our society and gave us steel towers and an indentured life. I've given them what they want. I *know* what they want, Cara. They want what everyone wants from me. Money, power. They want to *take* from me, and my family and my country. And I cannot let that happen. I will *always* defend the things that are important to me. No matter what."

"You're wrong."

"I'm not. You're naive. Everyone takes. *Everyone*. And it's my responsibility to defend my country, my people and my family from those takers. *Everyone* takes," he repeated, his voice low and dangerous.

Cara stepped away instinctively. It was as if a barrier had formed between them. Perhaps it had always been there and she'd preferred not to see it before. She shook her head. "Not everyone."

He didn't move, just kept watching her, as if he could hold her by his will alone. "*Listen* to me, Cara. Remember how I said you should trust me? Remember? *This* is what I meant. Yes, I wanted you away from the men. I had to. I had no other choice. I needed them busy for a couple of days. They wouldn't have believed me if I'd translated those words. They'd have been suspicious. But you?"

"*Yes. Me*. An insignificant little translator who couldn't possibly be partisan in any way. They'd believe me all right. Just as you wanted them to." She couldn't believe it. She'd been taken in yet again by a man who needed to use her peculiar blend of innocence and authority to make their schemes believable. She sat down as if she'd been knocked down. How could she have been so stupid? She got up again unsteadily, looking around for escape. "I have to go. I *need* to go."

"So my words to you this morning had no effect?"

"You still used me, whether or not you prepared me for this knowledge or not."

"I tried to explain *why* I used you."

"So you admit it?"

"Of course. There is little point in doing otherwise."

"And even as you were using me, you made love to me."

"No! Keeping you away from the Aurus executives was the reason I took you away, but *not* the reason I wanted to make love to you. You know that. In your heart, you *know* that."

And she did. She felt the truth of his words within her. Just as she felt the pain of his betrayal deep within her. She swallowed back the tears. "Tariq, why didn't you tell me?"

She saw a pain in his eyes she'd not detected before. "Cara, I couldn't tell you. There was too much at stake. I needed you innocent. If you'd known, and if you'd seen the men, your eyes would have betrayed you instantly. I couldn't risk it."

She stepped away. She felt his doubt, his distrust like acid in her throat. She swallowed it down. "No. Of course not. You couldn't trust me."

"I could only trust my brother."

She couldn't help remembering how closely he'd held her as he'd entered her, of the intimacy and mutual trust she'd believed they'd had in that moment. She hadn't doubted it then, but now she did.

She stepped away and he made no move towards her. "There was too much at stake. Don't you understand?"

Of course she did. It all made perfect sense. More than he

could know. She certainly couldn't be trusted and if he knew her better, he'd have known that. But it still hurt. She'd felt a connection with him that she'd never felt with anyone else. She nodded. "I understand."

She turned away from him, unable to continue to look into the eyes of the man she'd made love to again and again, over the last forty-eight hours. The eyes of a man who'd used her, just as other men in her life had. He was no different.

The hope and happiness that had bloomed, little by little over the past week, collapsed, forming a lumpen mass that felt like death. The hot air that blew in through the open window clogged her throat—she felt she couldn't breathe. She turned and walked away.

"Where are you going?"

She halted briefly but didn't turn to him. "Away. I believe my job here is finished. Isn't it? I've misled the Aurus executives, just as you wanted me to. I've served my purpose. I'm done!" She tried to make her voice as cold, as devoid of feeling as her heart felt, but she was afraid it wasn't. It sounded uneven and tremulous.

She jumped as she felt his hands on her arms. "Don't go yet, Cara, turn around, talk to me."

She shook her head again, as she felt a tear roll down her cheek. How could she turn around? Reveal her stupidity, her pathetic sadness at the discovery that he hadn't wanted her for herself, but only to use her for his own ends. Just like everyone else had her whole life through. "Let me go." Her voice trembled and his grip on her shoulders tightened. She waited for another command.

Instead, he let go of her shoulders and walked around, to face her.

"You're crying."

She closed her eyes and bit her lip to stop it from trembling. "It's what people do when they're hurt."

She forced herself to meet his gaze, despite the tears that welled in her eyes and tracked down her face. He swept his thumbs lightly across her cheeks, wiping them away.

"I'm sorry I hurt you."

And she could see he was. But it wasn't enough. "Not sorry enough to have done anything differently though."

"No. I'd do the same again, Cara. There was too much at risk."

She pushed away his arms. "Then there's no more to be said. I'll be on my way."

"I don't want you to go."

This imperious, illogical command was the last straw. Anger burned away any remaining sadness.

"Why? What possible reason could you have to want me to stay?" She was furious now. Furious that she'd been tricked, just as she had been in the past; furious that she'd allowed herself to be seduced by this man who only wanted to use her. Well, he might have used her, but there was no way she was going to behave like a used woman. "You might be King, you might be 'His Royal Highness, Sheikh Whatever', but I'm not your subject to command." She moved even closer to him, so that she had to look up into his eyes, frowning eyes, concerned eyes, hurt eyes. She shook her head. She didn't care if he was hurt. She had to take care of herself. "I'm nothing to you. You've proved that. So I'm going."

"To where?" His tone was bitter. "Back to Italy, or back to England, to the home you're so scared of? Where is it you really think you're going, Cara? Or don't you care, just so long as there is no rain to make you sad?" He pushed his fingers through her hair and held her head between his hands, trying to still her. She could feel the intensity in his fingers as he pressed against her skull, as if he wanted to get through to her, to connect with her physically, as he had in the desert. "Where?" His eyes bored into hers with an intensity bordering on desperation.

"Away," she whispered, aware of his lips so close to hers.

"Ah..." She watched his throat constrict and the tension in his fingers lessened as his hands slid from her head and he stepped back. "Away. You don't need anywhere to go to, so long as you're driven away. Away from me. Is that right? Because I didn't trust you, is that it? Or because you believe I betrayed the trust you put in me?"

The words of trust and betrayal swam in her mind—she could hardly make sense of them. The over-riding feeling was of a connection irrevocably broken. She needed to get away. She nodded, her heart too full to speak. "It doesn't matter. All that matters is that I'm going. You don't need me any more and you surely don't want me."

"Cara, I want you."

The meaning in his words turned her stomach to jelly. "You might want me, but you can't have me, Tariq."

"If you don't stay for me, then stay for Gadiel. He will be joining us shortly. Have you forgotten your promise to him to bring him books? Because he hasn't."

She closed her eyes as she remembered the previous day's promise to attend his birthday party and to give him books she'd treasured, had kept with her, from her childhood. They were in her bag. "Is this another one of your plans? You encouraged this arrangement yesterday when you knew how I'd be feeling today."

"I couldn't know how you'd be feeling. In fact, I hoped you'd be a little more... pragmatic, in your response."

"Pragmatic!" She was about to launch into a diatribe when there was a knock at the door and Gadiel entered the room, his eyes wide with excitement, his body language tense, as if unsure whether his entrance would be welcomed. There was no way she could leave now.

"Papa!" The boy walked up to Tariq who kissed his head, while the boy leaned in trustingly to his father.

Cara's heart ached at the love she could see between the two of them. The love that had somehow managed to survive their reserved natures, and the constraints being royal had imposed, was awkwardly expressed, but it was there.

"Miss Devlin!" The boy turned and walked quickly up to her and gave a small formal bow, as he'd obviously been taught. She felt a tug inside her and knew there was no way she could renege on her promise to him. "You didn't forget! Thank you for coming. Did you bring the books?"

She laughed, releasing the tension, and tousled the boy's hair. As if released from his formality he caught hold of her hand and gave her a disarming, gap-toothed grin. She sat down, opened her bag and pulled out the books of magic and mystery that had so charmed her as a little girl.

"Can we read them, now?"

She gave Tariq a quick look and then looked back at Gadiel. "Sure." She sat down and, without prompting he sat close beside her, his eyes wide as she leafed through the pages.

He pointed at one page and she stopped. He wriggled a little closer against her, so trustingly, so lovingly, that the lingering sense of bitterness lessened a little.

She didn't look up at Tariq but was aware of his silent presence as he watched her read to Gadiel. She continued to read, unable to stop herself from curling her arm around him, drawing him still closer to her. She allowed herself to be completely consumed by him and the story, pushing Tariq and all his complications out of her mind.

It was only when she'd reached the end of the story that she looked up to find Tariq hadn't gone, like she'd imagined. But was sitting across the room from them both, watching them silently.

The door opened and they could hear the festive shouts and laughter of children and adults mingling for the boy's birthday celebration. It was time for Gadiel to join them.

Gadiel jumped down and went running off into the other room, the book in his hands. He turned and waved to Cara. "Come and meet my friends!"

Cara and Tariq followed him towards the door. Before they emerged into the public gaze, Tariq stopped. "You've made quite an impression on my son."

"Yes, who'd have thought that I could inspire trust after such a brief acquaintance?"

The barb hit home. She could see it in the expression in his eyes as they ranged over her face as if he longed to touch her cheek, to kiss her eyelids, to place his lips upon hers. Then he stopped, clenched fists by his sides. "The sound of your voice instantly attracted me. It took me twenty-four hours to see how beautiful your eyes were, two days to appreciate the softness of your skin, after three days I understood, and was in awe of, your subtlety." He shook his head. "But trust? Trust is a different matter. I trusted my wife and she was unfaithful, I trusted my father and he betrayed me and my country. I don't know if I *can* trust again."

Without a backward glance he turned and walked into the room and was immediately swamped by family who cast curious looks her way. Of course. There would be no future with Tariq. Not just because he'd used her; not just because he hadn't trusted her, but because he was right not to.

After all, she was implicated in the biggest theft of ancient artifacts the country had ever known. And the evidence was sitting in her apartment.

CHAPTER 11

Tariq watched Cara play with his children at the party. Even Saarah was drawn to her now, watching her with the others, her face softening as she listened to Cara speak. Male or female, Cara's voice worked its magic. When he'd first heard it, he thought it a beautiful thing, something external to the woman herself. Now he knew he'd been wrong. It wasn't something separate to Cara, it was an expression of herself.

The children had got it straight away and had trusted her because of it. But he hadn't.

She turned her face and laughed at something Saarah said and Gadiel, who was so quiet and withdrawn, who was normally overlooked, flushed with her reaction and began talking animatedly as she quietly listened, nodding, encouraging. It was there in the boy's body language, as he shifted a little closer to her, his face lifting up to hers as he continued to talk. And she responded with the empathy that was such an important part of her.

Tariq turned as someone asked him a question and he nodded. Another decision: agreement to give something, approval to take something away—that was what was required of him. That was what he was accustomed to doing. So no wonder he'd been unprepared for this woman who wanted nothing, and who gave everything.

He turned back to her in time to see them all laugh at something his son had said. Even his eldest daughter's face lit up into a smile he'd not seen in years. Cara had brought life back to his family by simply being herself—selfless, honest and generous.

And he'd taken advantage of these qualities, had used her for his own ends—his country's own ends, he reminded himself. But for the first time in many years he doubted himself. He'd sacrificed his own happiness, and potentially that of his children, by deceiving this woman who stirred within him feelings that he'd never felt for anyone before.

When had it happened? He hadn't been aware of it. He could hardly think back to when he didn't know her, when he'd hardly noticed her when she'd appeared. He shook his head as if to rid it of its ignorance and stupidity. It seemed impossible now that she shouldn't be in his life.

A shaft of rich late afternoon sun slipped through the casement window, casting its glow on her pale hair, enflaming it, giving her the radiance that she occupied in his mind. She filled his vision and he knew, in that moment, that he couldn't let her walk out of his life. The thought of losing her now was untenable. He swallowed as real, true fear gripped his gut. He'd not had that feeling since he was a child and learned his mother had died. It had taken him years to screw that feeling up tight and bury it where he couldn't identify it.

He'd let no one close to his heart since, not even his children he suspected. But somehow Cara had eased into him—into every breath he took, had slipped under his skin and into every cell, every fiber of his being. For her to go would be to rip himself apart.

THE PARTY HAD ENDED and the children had left, and still Tariq kept his distance. People drifted away. Cara turned and went to collect her abaya, the same red silk as the dress Tariq had given her. She wrapped it around her shoulders and smoothed down the expensive cloth.

She'd felt beautiful wearing it. More than that, *Tariq* had made her feel beautiful. And yet, all the while he'd been using her.

She walked over to the window and looked outside into the garden, now flooded with the orange light of sunset. It was so beautiful. A beautiful garden, in a beautiful country, surely worth saving for its people, at any price? Even the price of her pride?

And she'd been using him, too, hadn't she? She glanced at her watch. It would soon be time for her to leave. Not just the palace, but Ma'in. She'd written a letter to Tariq, and all she had to do now was to package up the statue and arrange for the courier to deliver them after she'd left the country.

It was nearly done. Time was running out.

"Cara!"

Startled, she turned around to face Tariq. "Please, come with me." He glanced around, uncharacteristically edgy.

"I was just leaving. I've a plane to catch later tonight."

Some emotion flared in his eyes—whether it was anger, fear or need, she couldn't have said—but it was contained as he pressed his lips together and simply nodded. "I would have a few words in private, in my office, before you leave."

Did he suspect something? No, he wouldn't be so calm if he knew the truth.

They walked to his office, with its windows on all sides, windows which from the outside appeared like mirrors.

"You can see forever here."

He came up behind her and followed her gaze around the busy foyer below where visitors and officials mingled. Beyond the foyer, the high windows looked out onto the gardens and beyond that to the sea one way, and to the desert and distant mountains the other.

"We can see forever, and no one can see us. A private view."

"That's what you do, isn't it? Observe and care for everyone, for your whole world, while you stay apart, unobserved, private... *safe*."

He shook his head, a smile lifting his usually stern lips. "We've known each other such a short time. And yet you appear to know me better than anyone else."

She shrugged. "I doubt it. They're just my impressions."

"*Correct* impressions. I do keep myself safe. Usually. When I can see things coming, I make sure I'm safe. But I didn't see *you* coming."

She looked around, startled by his words.

"Cara, I'm sorry..."

"You used me, Tariq. But I understand why you did."

Tariq sighed and reached for her, pulling her to him. "I'm so sorry. I had no choice. The stakes were too high. I had to resolve this situation. For my people, for my country. And for me."

"It's okay." And it *was* okay on one level, even though the hurt continued beneath that thinking, pragmatic level. "This is your world. You're a part of it and you needed to defend it in any way you could. Unfortunately you chose a woman who was tired of being used."

"Who used you?"

There was something in his expression, as if he'd hunt

down the people and deal with them, that made her smile. He was so much the leader, the alpha male who felt responsible for everything that befell his people. And, for whatever reason, it now seemed he viewed her as one of his people.

"It doesn't matter now."

"If it still matters to you, it matters to me. Tell me."

"My mother first. She didn't mean to, but she needed me. I was more like a parent to my mother, than a daughter. She was so gifted and yet so unbalanced. My father was her rock and when he wasn't around I had to be. She couldn't cope after he died. And then... well. I guess I'd set a pattern for myself."

"A pattern we can break. *Now*. I promise I'll never use you or your talents again, for any purpose whatsoever. Do you believe me?"

She nodded. She *did* believe him. The truth was there in his eyes. In the way he brushed her cheek with his thumbs, caressing her as if he genuinely cherished her. "Yes, I believe you."

"Good. Cara, you must stay."

"I can't. I have to go. I'm booked on the flight to England tonight. I have things to sort out."

"Forget that. I know we've not known each other long, but I don't want you to leave."

She could hardly believe what she was hearing. He was the King of his country. So upright, he'd never brought a woman to meet his children in the two years since his wife's death. "You mean you have another job for me?"

He smiled. "You're being obtuse now. You know I don't mean that."

"I need to hear exactly what you mean."

"Exactly? Well, I was going to disguise my full intent, for as long as I could, so as not to frighten you off. But here goes. I want you to marry me, Cara. I can't imagine a life without you. I love you and don't want you to leave my side. I want you to be with me always."

"Marry?" she whispered.

"I want to marry you. I know we've known each other for a short time only, but I don't need any more time to know what I want. And it's *you*. I don't want to marry you here, not today. But I want you to return to Ma'in as soon as you can. Then, I will show you my country properly. Then, you will get to know my children slowly. Then, I will make you love me as much as I love you."

She swallowed back the tide of emotion that threatened to drown any remaining shreds of reason she had. She wanted to tell him that she already loved him. But how could she tell him that when tomorrow morning he'd discover just why exactly she couldn't marry him. And… why he wouldn't want her. She had to stop this. It couldn't go anywhere.

"Tariq, I…"

He pressed his finger against her lips. "Don't answer me yet."

She gasped against his finger and closed her eyes, as she tried to contain her arousal at his touch.

"Don't," he whispered again, closer to her now. She kissed his finger. Then he tugged it away and replaced it with his lips. But this was no gentle touch, his mouth captured hers in a kiss which contained all the passion she'd heard in his voice and seen in his eyes.

And she responded. She had no choice. Her hands were about his body as her mouth and tongue tangled with his. He pressed himself against her and she shifted, accommodating his shape to her own, opening her legs around his.

They moved back until she was pressed against the glass that overlooked the whole of the downstairs foyer where people walked back and forth, talking in groups, unaware and unable to see what was happening high above them.

Her hands gripped the cloth of his shirt and slid underneath onto his body, the muscles hard and taut and strong, as his hands pulled up her dress, moving over and cupping her bottom, bringing her up to him. She parted her legs, curling them around his hips as her sex rubbed against his hard erection.

She wanted him inside her, for one last time. Wanted to feel what he could make her feel. "Tariq. I want you. But here? What if someone should come in?"

Tariq was on fire with lust. "No one would dare, Cara. *No one.* It's just you and me. Let me show you how much I want you to stay. Let me show you how much I care for you."

She twisted around in his arms. "But, out there." She looked down at all the people moving around, purposeful, oblivious to the scene being played out above them.

"Perfect. You've lived your life in private, in the shadows. Look out there."

She turned to face the window and he moved his hand up under her dress, undressing her, feeling her. She closed her eyes and trembled under his touch. She groaned and shifted her bottom back towards him, allowing his fingers greater access to the place he wanted to be. He swiftly undid his fly.

"Open your eyes, Cara. I want to show the world that you're mine. I *want* you to feel exposed." With that, he lifted her against him and he rubbed himself against her. She was wet and ready for him. "You will be my wife, my Queen. *This* will be your world."

She rested her head on her arms, against the wall of glass, and reached behind, feeling him, urging him on, pushing herself out to him. He needed no more invitation and he plunged deep inside her, her body slick and welcoming. She cried out in surprise with an instant orgasm that drove him on harder.

Her panting, her whimpers, her moans grew louder and

then she cried out his name, falling against the steel rail that ran around the window, needing its support, as he continued to thrust, until his world went white and he came into her, pumping his seed, making sure she received it at her center.

Slowly he came aware of the world around him once more. He could hardly believe the power of his orgasm, of her power over him. He withdrew from her and held her in his arms, turning her to face him. She filled his vision. The world was at his feet but all he could see was her.

He drew her hard against him, kissing her hair that smelled of apricots. He kissed her neck and groaned as he felt himself become aroused once more at the smell and feel of her. Everything about her was like an aphrodisiac to him. He couldn't get enough. He doubted he'd *ever* get enough. "Tell me what you're thinking."

She opened her mouth but no words emerged immediately. Then she turned and whispered something.

"What did you say?" He'd heard but he wanted her to say it louder.

"That I *love*… making love to you."

"I've never known anyone like you, Cara. You're so honest, so straightforward. Most people want something from me, but you? Maybe you do want something." He smiled. "But what you want is something I want to give. That honesty is unusual in my world Cara, and I value it."

She pulled away, a frown resting above her green eyes. "No one's perfect. Least of all me. Everyone has a past, even me."

He smiled but she didn't. "Even you, Cara?" He searched her face, smiling, trying to understand the sudden seriousness. "Of course you have a past. Nobody arrives fully formed but I trust you, trust your innocence your honesty, like I've never trusted anyone before."

"Tariq, I—"

AWAKENED BY THE SHEIKH

He hushed her words with a kiss. "Don't try to prove otherwise, Cara, because I shan't believe you." He didn't understand where her thoughts were going but he knew how to bring her back to him.

"Tariq"—she pulled away—"I have to go."

"I don't want you to go."

"I have to. My plane leaves later tonight."

"I'll only let you go if you promise to return. I was serious about wanting us to get married."

She bit her lip and the frown returned. Why didn't she answer?

"Will you?"

She shifted away, not meeting his eye. "Marry you? You hardly know me. Besides," she spluttered, "you're the King, I'm… nobody."

"Never say that! Cara, listen to me. The first time I married it wasn't for love; it was an arranged marriage to a woman my family deemed 'suitable'. I never loved my wife, I hardly respected her for the choices she made, but she was a good mother to my children and she's now dead. I did not intend to marry again but then I saw you and little by little I've fallen for you. I didn't even realize it to begin with. You've slipped under my skin, breached my defenses, without me being aware of it. Cara, I want you to marry me. Will you?"

"Tariq, no…I…" She looked him in the eye but he wasn't reassured by the expression he saw there. "No. I can't. There are so many reasons why I can't."

"Marry me, Cara. Forget who I am, forget the world I live in. I'm just a man who's fallen in love with a woman I didn't even know existed. I can't believe I've found you, and I cannot live without you. Look at me, Cara."

But she continued to look out into the distant sky.

"Marry me," he repeated, demanding rather than asking now, as the desperation and fear ate away at his certainty.

"I can't, Tariq."

"When you return here from England, we'll take our time. I'll woo you, court you, if you like. I realize we haven't known each other long. We'll spend time together, get to know each other better."

"I can't," she repeated.

He could hardly believe what he was hearing. "Cara, what do I have to say to make you see? Don't you feel the way our bodies fit, the way our minds and feelings meld together so perfectly? We belong together."

"Tariq, I can't marry you. It's that simple."

"Okay. I understand. We've not known each other long. Just because I'm certain, it doesn't mean you are. I'll give you time."

"No. You're not listening to me, Tariq."

"I know our cultures are different. You are from England and I'm from Ma'in but—"

"Tariq! I *can't* marry you, not I *don't want* to!"

Sick. He felt sick as comprehension dawned on him. He withdrew his hands from her. "Tell me why."

She licked dry lips. "I'm already married."

CHAPTER 12

Tariq jerked away from her and pushed his hands through his hair, shaking his head.

"Tariq! I'm sorry. It's not as it seems."

She reached out her hand to him but he jumped up at her touch and walked away.

"Tariq! Look at me. Talk to me."

"You *demand* I talk to you? You accuse me of not trusting you? And yet, all along you are *married*?" He shook his head, the hurt in his eyes cutting her to the bone. "You're unbelievable."

"I'm married only because I haven't yet been able to get a divorce. I'm married in name only. It's been this way for over a year."

But still the look of pain and incomprehension filled his face. Tears sprung to her eyes. "Tariq!" she half-sobbed. "You have to believe me, it's over in all but name." He turned away from her. "A piece of paper, that's all it is!"

He walked to the bathroom and closed the door behind him.

"Tariq," she called through the door. "Let me explain. Let

me tell you everything." She knocked on the bathroom door. There was no answer. She tried the handle and the door opened. He hadn't locked it. She went inside. He was leaning, hands gripping the basin, head down. She walked up behind him and placed a tentative hand on his shoulder. "Tariq, let me explain."

He looked up at her in the mirror. "I don't need an explanation. What I need, Cara, is for you to leave. You've a plane to catch, remember?"

"I remember. But we should talk first."

He grunted. "I don't think so." And walked back into his office. She followed behind. She had to get through to him. She approached tentatively and placed a hand on his arm. He simply looked down at her hand until she removed it. He picked up his phone and began flicking through his emails.

"Tariq! I can't leave you like this!"

He turned fully towards her for the first time, anger flowing from him in waves. "Why can't you? It's over. You've got what you wanted from me—whatever that was—and now it's time for you to go. That's what you planned isn't it? Now you have to return to your husband."

"It's not like that."

"Then what *is* it like?"

"He married me for one reason only. To use me."

"How did he use you?"

Should he tell him now? What if he didn't believe her innocence? "He…" she half-sobbed, "I…"

"Don't bother. I'm not interested. The only thing I'm curious about is how the woman I'd come so close to, could have deceived me so well." He sighed and thrust his fingers through his hair.

"I—"

He held up his hand. "And you can't tell me the answer. It's my fault. I let my guard slip. *Stupid*."

She flexed her hands which ached to hold him, to make him listen to her. But there was no way she could force a man like Tariq to do anything. "I'm sorry, Tariq. I guess I should have told you before."

He froze, still not looking at her. "You guess?"

She shrugged. "It wasn't something that had come up. I mean, when should I have told you?"

He turned slowly to her then and looked at her with eyes that she didn't recognize—they were cold, hard, hidden. "You don't know when you should have told me? How about before I kissed you? Or even after I kissed you? Even if you thought nothing of that, maybe you should have told me before we made love, don't you think?"

"You're right, of course you're right. But it's not so easy. There are... other matters which complicate things."

"And what is so complicated about marriage? It's simple. You are a wife. You have a husband. You should be faithful to that husband. *That*, Cara, is what marriage is to me. But obviously not to you."

She backed away, hating the bitterness in his voice, hating the anger and hurt in his eyes and most of all, hating why she couldn't defend his accusations.

"I was your employee. I had no idea things would escalate like this!"

"Escalate? We fell for each other. You knew my wife died two years ago and I assumed you were single. You never suggested anything to the contrary. You agreed you had 'no significant other.'"

"And I haven't. Listen to me, Tariq. I'm married in name only."

Tariq's laugh was bitter. He turned back to her. "'In name only'. And what exactly is that meant to mean? *I* was married in name only. A marriage is a marriage. You sign a piece of paper and you're officially married. And if you are married you do *not* have sex with other people. *That* is disloyal. That is *not* acceptable."

"Hey, don't go around telling me what's right and what's wrong. You don't know the full story."

"The full story you refuse to tell me, you mean?" He stood over her, a muscle flickering in his jaw betraying the struggle that was revealed in his eyes. He was close to her now and she watched as the expression in his eyes turned from bitterness to a hurt that was palpable.

"I'm so sorry, Tariq. Hurting you is the last thing I want to do. Being with you has been the most important thing in my life."

"Then tell me everything."

"I can't. I simply can't. Not yet. It's complicated." She paused. "You'll know soon."

"You don't trust me with this?"

"It's not that—"

"You don't trust me?" he repeated.

"I *can't* trust you."

"Then that's enough said." He stepped away again. "My children wished to say goodbye to you. I will allow this because I don't wish them to be hurt by your non-appearance. Go there now and I'll have a driver take you to wherever you want to go, afterwards."

He closed the door with a deliberateness that sent an icy shiver right to her heart. A sudden burst of anger overtook her and she slapped the palms of her hands on the door, wanting to open it and shout after him. But how did you shout that she had never loved her husband? How did you shout that she loved *him*, Tariq? How did she shout that she couldn't tell him because once Tariq knew her secrets he'd no longer want her?

As soon as Cara walked into the family sitting room, her heart stopped. Standing with his back to her, outlined by the light was Tariq. Then she saw the children laughing and the silhouette moved and turned to her with a welcoming smile. It wasn't Tariq. Just someone who looked like him.

She must have looked shocked because the man walked towards her with a concerned look on his face. "Are you okay?"

"Sure. Sorry, I just wasn't expecting anyone other than the children."

"Nor were they." He grinned and extended his hand to hers. "I'm Sahmir, Tariq's youngest brother and you must be the Cara I've heard so much about."

"Yes." She shook his hand. "Tariq said you were in Paris."

"Yes. I'm back earlier than anticipated."

"Did you have a good trip?" she asked politely, trying desperately to think of something to say to Ma'in's glamorous Prince, while all she could think about was Tariq.

He grimaced. "Shall we say 'interesting'? Care for a drink?"

"Please. A coffee would be great."

He poured two coffees and returned to the table.

"Uncle Sahmir! Come back and play."

"Later! Where are your manners?" But his tone was light.

"Please, don't let me stop you from playing with your nieces and nephew."

"I'll play with them later. Besides, I don't often get a chance to talk to a woman Tariq has introduced to his children."

Cara lowered her eyes and took a sip of the hot, black coffee. She felt exhausted, drained and didn't relish getting the third degree from Tariq's brother.

"I believe you employed me, Your Royal Highness."

"Call me Sahmir. And yes, I did employ you. I have to admit, I fell for your voice on the chocolate ad. And…"

"And you imagined me to be a femme fatale who would entertain your brother for a few weeks." She took another sip, watching Sahmir through amused, narrowed eyes. "Give him some light relief from his work."

"Um, looks like you can see right through me. But I have to say"—he leaned forward, resting his arms on his knees as he grinned disarmingly at her—"my plan seems to have worked."

She opened her mouth to speak, tempted to confide everything to this stranger. But he was Tariq's brother. She bit her lip. "I'm leaving in a few hours."

He raised his eyebrows in surprise. "Ah, so maybe it didn't work as well as I'd imagined. Shame. So… where are you headed?"

"England."

"For a holiday?"

"Just a week or so to tie up some loose ends and then I'm moving to Italy."

He pressed his lips together in regret. "That really *is* a shame."

She shrugged, trying to look casual. She was sure it didn't come off. She wasn't that good an actress. "No, it's not. There's nothing to keep me here."

He rose. "Not even Tariq?"

She rose too. "Especially not Tariq."

Just at that moment the children saw her through the open double doors. "Cara!"

Sahmir gave a low whistle and looked from Cara back to the children. "On first name terms with Tariq's children?" He watched with interest as Eshal toddled up to Cara and attached herself to her leg, as Cara petted her head. "On more than first name terms with Eshal!" He laughed and gathered the girl in his arms, twisting her around until she was shrieking with laughter.

When the children had been successfully diverted, Cara took the opportunity of asking the question she most wanted the answer to.

"So have you seen Tariq in the last hour?" She'd tried to make her voice casual, as if it were simply a polite enquiry, but, judging by the smile on Sahmir's face, she hadn't succeeded. "Is… is he okay?"

"Not that I want to pry," he shrugged, "although I probably do, but why do you think Tariq wouldn't be okay?" he asked.

"Just wondered."

"All right. You're as discreet as Tariq, I get it. Even if you do give more away in your eyes than he does. Anyway, I don't know how he is. I haven't seen him yet. I'm putting off the evil moment when I introduce him to a… a lady who's with me."

"Your fiancee? Tariq told me you were getting engaged on your return."

"*He* told you that?"

"Sorry, I didn't think. No doubt it's private, family stuff. He only mentioned it in passing."

"That's okay. It's just that Tariq rarely talks about family matters to anyone outside the family. He must have trusted you."

She shrugged, trying to hide the pain of the misguided compliment.

"So where is she? Your fiancee?"

"She's not actually my fiancee. She's freshening up. She's had a hell of a week and she's resting before it's topped off by my brother's displeasure."

It was Cara's turn to be confused. "Why would Tariq be

displeased with meeting your fiancee-to-be? He was expecting her."

"The lady who's with me, isn't the woman I was meant to marry."

"Oh!" It seemed Tariq's brother was nothing like Tariq. "And Tariq doesn't know yet?"

Sahmir gave an embarrassed, rueful grin. "No, not yet. He seems to have disappeared without trace. Even Aarif doesn't know where he is." He raised an eyebrow. "Have you any idea?"

She shook her head.

"Any clue as to his mood?"

It was her turn to grimace. "Not a good one, I'm afraid."

"Oh. You, too?"

She nodded. "It was my fault. I neglected to tell him something important."

"Couldn't have been that important."

"Oh, yes, it was." She wanted to tell this stranger everything she couldn't tell Tariq. It was ridiculous. What good would it do? She'd be away shortly and her time with Tariq would be only a dream. But… she didn't want it to be a dream.

"You can tell me, you know. I'm the extrovert brother; Tariq's the introvert and Daidan? Well, only Allah knows what Daidan is."

"He's in Finland, I understand?"

"Yes. In the cold snowy north, mining diamonds. He's even worse than Tariq when it comes to emotional stuff." He leaned forward. "So tell me what it was you should have told him. Maybe I can help."

"Thank you, but nothing can help. I'm married, you see. To a man who doesn't love me, and who I don't love. We've not been 'together' for over a year now. And I haven't known where he was for some of that time so I haven't been able to get a divorce."

"And you told Tariq that?"

"Some of it, but he wouldn't listen."

"Of course he wouldn't." She waited for him to continue but he suddenly looked distracted. "Look, I have to go and sort a few things out. Hope to see you later." He rose and kissed her hand. "Lovely to meet you, Cara. I hope we meet again."

Before Cara could tell him she'd be leaving and wouldn't be seeing him again, he was gone.

Saying goodbye to the children was harder than she'd thought. Despite the few times she'd seen them she'd grown attached to them. Gadiel, in particular, had been difficult to leave. He'd wanted to know when he'd see her again. It had only been the reappearance of his nurse who'd saved her.

As she walked through the palace foyer, she realized she'd never see Tariq again. By tomorrow morning, she'd be gone and he'd have opened the courier package, containing the statue that would tell him everything. She looked around at its grandeur and opulence and realized with a shock that she felt none of the awe she'd experienced when she'd first entered the palace. Rather, she shared Tariq's feelings that too high a price had been paid for it all.

Finally she glanced up at the opaque windows where his office was. She'd been up there just hours before. She continued walking, desperate not to relive that time. Not yet. That would be for later.

The same guards who'd tried to bar her access now nodded respectfully to her as she left the building. A driver immediately approached and took her to a car with tinted windows, waiting under the shaded portico at the foot of the steps. Only the best for her now, she thought wryly.

She got into the car and found herself face to face with

Tariq and slammed herself back against the seat in surprise. "Tariq!"

"I'm sorry to have startled you."

"What are you doing here?"

"I wanted a few words in private." He turned to the driver and pressed the intercom. "Take us to Miss Devlin's apartment." He gave him the address. He sat back and observed her coolly.

"Look, Tariq, if you've come here to harangue me again, forget it. What's done's done and—"

"I know—"

"There's nothing…" She snapped her head around to face him. "You know? *What* do you know?"

"That there's nothing that can be done with the past. It's been explained to me in no uncertain terms that you are the right woman for me and that I mustn't let you get away. Married or not."

"What?" Cara gasped. "Who told you that?"

"My little brother. He's always been, shall we say, more adept at things of the heart."

"Sahmir told you?" She remembered his sudden disappearance. "Ah."

"You obviously made quite an impression."

"It would be the first time."

"My brother is a connoisseur of women and, as such, is a very good judge of character. A trait he prefers to keep quiet. And he's right. You are the right woman for me. But, as it happened, his advice wasn't required. I was on my way to see you."

Guilt flooded Cara. "Tariq, I need to tell you something."

"No, you don't. I know all there is to know, now. I just want you to know I'm sorry for how I behaved. I was taken by surprise. And I'm not good with surprises."

"I'm so sorry, Tariq. I never imagined, for one moment,

that our relationship would develop like it did. You just need to know that there are valid reasons I didn't tell you about my marriage. If you ask me in one month's time whether I'm married or not, the answer will be 'no'. I'd tell you that I *was* married but that I'm now divorced. And happily so. Though while we were living as man and wife, I want you to know that I was never disloyal, not in thought, nor fact."

He nodded. "And you will come back here, when you've finished your business in England? When you're divorced?"

She knew that by then Tariq would have discovered the whole story and wouldn't want her anyway. "If you still want me to, then yes." That, was the truth at least.

"Good. I want you to now. And there's nothing that will make me change my mind."

He pulled her towards him in a kiss that was meant as a reconciliation, but that turned into something far more passionate. It seemed that every time they came close now, their bodies wanted far more from each other. But now was not the time, nor place.

The car stopped before their kiss. It was Tariq who drew away first. "We're here."

"Here?" she repeated, unable to think where 'here' was immediately. Then she remembered. Her apartment. She suddenly had a vision of the statue, still placed on the window sill of her apartment.

"I can come upstairs, if you've time?"

She shook her head, lowering her eyes, trying to hide her panic. He thought he knew everything he needed to know about her. He was wrong. If he came upstairs there was a risk he'd see the statue and he'd never believe that she'd arranged for it to be returned to him if he found it upstairs, now.

"I'm sorry. I need to finish packing."

He pressed his forehead to hers, his hand caressing her cheek. "I don't want you to go."

"And I don't want to go. But I need to sort out a few things in England and then, if you want me to come to you, call me."

"I want you to come. You don't need further proof surely."

"I do." She turned away and then stepped out of the door, opened by the chauffeur. She bobbed her head down to look into the car, one last time, intent on imprinting the image of his face she'd come to love so much into her brain, so she'd never forget it. The dark eyes usually so inscrutable, but with her, so open, so expressive, just as they were now, and his lips, lips that knew how to arouse her body to heights she'd never before experienced… and never would again. "Goodbye, Tariq. And thank you."

He was about to speak when she turned and ran into the building, not trusting herself to stay. The cool of the air conditioning was welcome as the hot tears tracked down her face. She entered one of the waiting elevators, without talking to the concierge. She slumped against the wall, punching in the code that would take her straight into her apartment, and sobbed for a life gone wrong. It felt as if she'd been on a train her whole life, surging forward, endlessly making one wrong decision after another until she found herself here—with the opportunity of love with a good man in a country she adored, only for it to turn to dust.

The elevator stopped in her vestibule and she walked across the small, elegant space and entered the living room. All that was left were her open suitcases and one statue, sitting on the deep window sill, outlined against the brilliant blue of the sky.

She threw the last remaining things into her suitcase, closed it and then adjusted the position of the statue on the window sill—the only thing left in the room. This was her last task, to package up the statue and send it, together with a letter she'd labored over, via courier to Tariq. By the time he received it she'd be long gone.

Then she heard a ping of the elevator and her heart stopped. She couldn't move as the elevator doors opened and Tariq thanked the concierge and stepped out in the vestibule and walked through the open door to where she stood, rooted to the spot.

The smile that initially sprung to his face froze and fell with shock when he saw the statue.

"What the…?" He walked over to it, touching it, shaking his head as he looked first at her and then back to the statue. "Cara?" She swallowed a sob at the look of total devastation on his face. "Tell me what it's doing here?"

She swallowed. "My husband…" She cleared her throat. "My husband, Piers… he… stole it."

"Your… *husband*." He practically spat out the name. "Cara, if you're trying to destroy me, you're succeeding. Was my heart not enough?" He picked up the statue. "Thousands of years old. A part of my heritage. A heritage you and your husband set out to steal when you came to Ma'in. My heart, Cara, and my identity. You want both of those things, that I've tried so hard to protect."

"I was leaving the statue for you. You must believe me."

"Must I?"

If anger, rather than despair had filled his face, she might have been better able to handle it. She rummaged through her handbag looking for the letter she'd written him. She plucked it out and held it to him. "Here, read it. You see the wrapping? I was about to put it together and have it sent to you. I couldn't tell you before because I was scared. Scared you wouldn't believe me. Scared you'd put me behind bars."

"You are a traitor to this country, and to me. Cara, I never want to see you again. I'll have Aarif escort you out of the country, to make sure you leave."

He picked up the statue without taking the letter of explanation from her hands and walked back to the elevator which immediately sprang open for him. Cara couldn't have said if he'd turned around as the doors closed behind him, for one last glimpse of the woman who he'd given his heart to, and who'd betrayed everything he held dear. She couldn't have said because the room spun and everything went black.

CHAPTER 13

Two Months Later. Norfolk, England.

It was Cara's favorite time of day. She stretched out her feet and placed them on the rickety table beside the plot of geraniums She'd been on the computer all day so it felt good to sit outside on her apartment's small balcony, projecting out over the shop below, and relax.

Despite her work, she hadn't felt alone. The bustling bakery above which she worked and lived kept her supplied with company in the form of her oldest friend when she needed it, delicious pastries which she certainly shouldn't have snacked on, and above all the feel that she was part of a family. Even if she wasn't.

Resting her arms along the black-painted ironwork of the balustrade, she peered down into the busy street below. The village was quieter than usual. It was mid week and, with the sky dark toward the south, with the promise of thunder, there were few tourists around.

From the balcony, Cara could see the huge gates behind which lay the remains of the Priory. Trees barely moved in the hot, humid, still air. There was a sense of expectation. She shivered, but not from the old sense of foreboding thunder storms gave her—that had gone.

The last few months had been hectic, setting up her new internet translation business, settling into a village she'd only known a little from her visits to her grandmother's house and, not least, getting a divorce.

She waved in response to the owner of the grocery shop opposite, who had unhooked his striped canvas awning, ready to close up for the day. "Enjoy the last of the sun," he called. "Looks like it'll pour down soon."

"I will." She called back. "And thanks for the apples!"

"My pleasure. Have a good evening!" And he was gone.

Despite the threat of rain, Cara stood up and looked down the street, first one way and then another. Five thirty pm and the shops were now all shut up with only the soft thud of music coming from the restaurant two doors down. The air seemed unusually breathless and heavy. Despite the threat of rain—or even because of it—she thought she'd go for a walk, after all.

WITH THE LARGE entrance gates now closed for the day, Cara slipped into the Abbey grounds through a small gate at the back of the monastery, used by locals, and hidden from the curious by overgrown trees and bushes. She walked under the barely moving canopy of the massive oaks, towards the soaring expanse of the eastern window of the Abbey—the only surviving remains of the Augustinian Priory. She walked beyond it to where the Abbey woods ended and a low fence gave way to a field of unmoving gold, spilling down the gentle hill toward the setting sun. She closed her eyes against the light, imagining she was back in Ma'in. But she couldn't. The light here was so different to the sun in

Ma'in. But she kept her eyes closed, allowing her thoughts to move back in time, back to Tariq, back to what might have been.

To begin with, she'd tried hard not to remember. But she couldn't help it. She tried to keep in the present while she was in her apartment, but here was her secret place, where she could remember.

Remember his stern eyes that turned passionate when they looked at her; remember the way he said her name, with the accent on the 'r' rather than the 'a', and remembered the feel of his lips and body pressed to hers.

She remembered everything about him as if he were a part of her.

A fork of lightning split the sky. She opened her eyes to see the sun had completely disappeared behind an ominous wall of iron grey cloud. There was no rain yet and it was still warm so she idly counted the seconds until thunder crashed and rolled around the village and wide fields.

She should go back to her apartment, maybe finish off the work she'd begun late this afternoon, go through her accounts. There was always something to keep her busy. But for some reason she didn't move. Somehow she felt closer to him here.

She watched as the dark clouds moved across the fields towards her and remembered how it had rained for weeks without ending after her father and mother had died. And for years afterwards, she'd hated the rain, hated the feelings of helplessness and grief it reminded her of.

But that had all changed with Tariq. Loving him had enabled her to see beyond the grief, made her able to return to the only place that had felt like home to her, growing up, rather than keep on running.

Suddenly the rain was upon her. She looked up to see the oak leaves twitching under the firm drops of rain that heralded the onslaught. These were quickly followed by a deluge and a rumble of thunder that echoed all around.

She turned her face up to the sky. Rain like this was practically worshipped in Ma'in. She laughed as the torrent of rain quickly soaked her hair, and remembered the rain storm she and Tariq had encountered in the desert. She pulled her arms around her body and pressed her palm to her gut. *Remembering. Wanting.*

But the pain was too much and she turned and retraced her steps, still pressing a hand to her stomach: the feelings, visceral and strong. It was only when she returned to the cobbled street opposite her apartment that she stopped and leaned against the old flint wall that surrounded the monastery, and took shelter under the overhanging lilac, whose scent filled the air.

She looked up at her three-storied apartment, so quaint and pretty above the medieval shop fronts. This was her reality now. She had to let go. Reluctantly, she withdrew her hand, her hand that was *his* hand, and thought of him for one last time.

Another crack of thunder and, with her eyes scrunched so tight, with her heart pounding at the memory, she could almost hear the way Tariq said her name, as if it was something soft and beautiful… as if *she* was beautiful.

Cara… when he looked at her with a surprised expression as if he had only just noticed something about her.

Cara… when he touched her cheek gently with the tip of his finger, frowning in puzzlement.

Cara… when he whispered in her ear in complete mastery and satisfaction, as his body eased into her.

Cara! She opened her eyes abruptly, torn from her reverie by a sharpening of sound, and looked out to the road between her and her apartment. There was someone standing under her balcony, a dark shape. What the…? She peered into the gloom. There was a flash of lightning and she saw a single, solitary figure standing in front of her door, drenched to the skin like her, his eyes, intense, looking as if he wanted to devour her.

"Tariq?" she whispered, hardly able to speak through a suddenly dry mouth. She raked her fingers up through her hair, gripping her head, trying to contain the shock, straining into the darkening light to see if he was real or a figment of her imagination. Was it a dream? Had she somehow summoned him up out of her imagination, out of the urgent desires of her heart?

Another flash of lightning lit the scene with an eerie silver light. It *was* him! In the gloom that followed all she could see was the now torrential rain bouncing off his black coat, that flapped in the wind the storm had stirred.

He seemed like an avenging angel, or a dark harbinger of bad news.

What had he come here for? To give, or to take away? Whatever it was, she had to find out.

She ran through the torrential rain, over the uneven cobbled road, to him, her eyes fixed on his. "Tariq?"

His face changed in an instant, as if his own disbelief had been suddenly vanquished. A smile flickered into his eyes and then radiated out to his cheeks and mouth. It was always that way with him. As if his face was unwilling to betray his feelings. But they did now. With her. "Are you going to stand there getting soaked, staring at me, or may I come inside?"

She jumped to the door, her hands trembling as she tried to unlock it. "Sure. Sure." She finally got the key in the lock and turned to look at him once more, needing to be reassured he was still there. "Tariq? Is it *really* you?"

That grin again, so uncommon that it tore straight to her heart and held it. "Do you have many people standing in the pouring rain, waiting for you to appear?"

She grinned back, trying to hold back the knot of emotion that threatened to make her voice wobble. "They usually form an orderly queue, not yell across the road to me."

"Then, they are not men. Now, open the door, and let me in!"

Laughing she opened the door wide and he followed her through the hallway that ran alongside the bakery and then up the stairs, the old-fashioned rods that held in the carpet runners clacking under her flip flops.

Wordlessly, she stepped aside and he walked into the hall. She'd never particularly noticed the small dimensions of the medieval building before. But now, Tariq filled it. Why was he here? She wanted to know, and yet didn't want to know, just in case it was the wrong answer. She tried to smile. "Welcome to my world."

He raised his eyebrows. "And what a welcome. I always thought you were some kind of witch, changing the weather with a sleight of hand, luring innocent men to their doom with your siren voice." He licked his lips and she noticed that his eyes were focused on hers. She snatched in a suddenly elusive breath.

"Well, the siren voice now offers you warmth and refreshment. Follow me."

Why had she asked him to follow her? She was acutely aware of the short shorts she wore, her bare legs and tight t-shirt. He'd think her scruffy and ill-dressed.

She walked across to the kitchen area and put on the kettle. She turned her head but didn't look at him. "Coffee?"

"Please."

She filled the Arabic coffee pot with water, added some finely ground Arabic coffee, a spoon of sugar and turned on the heat. She went to the bathroom and plucked a towel from the rack and took it to him.

"I think you need this as much as me." He gave the towel back to her.

She stepped away. "I'm fine. I'll go and change." She plucked at the scruffy t-shirt that had seen too many washes, particularly with red socks. "I wasn't expecting company, so… shorts"—she flashed him a quick awkward grin—"and… flip flops." She looked into his eyes which narrowed in confusion. "I work from home, so…"

She stopped abruptly. The words froze on her lips and he didn't break the silence. He simply lifted his hand and pushed a soaking lock of hair behind her ear. "You look… just right."

It was her turn to frown. Just *right*? Just right for what? She guessed at least he wasn't being critical. But then the stir of feminine vanity made her feel that if it was meant to be a compliment it was severely lacking. She smiled briefly in confusion, and turned and fled to her bedroom where she peeled off her wet clothes and plucked a dress out of the wardrobe. Her mind was racing. Why had he returned?

She quickly dried her hair, swept a comb through it and re-entered the lounge. She stopped suddenly, arrested by the sight of him. He'd taken off his coat and stood in a crumpled white shirt and casual trousers, his dark skin looking even darker against the white. A few chest hairs curled against the edge of the shirt. He was studying one of her framed family photographs in his hands.

She hurried into the kitchen, added the cardamom to the frothing coffee, took a deep breath and walked back into the lounge.

She held out the coffee to him. He seemed to sense her discomfort and smiled before taking the coffee.

"Coffee and cups from Ma'in," he said approvingly, smelling its aroma. He glanced up at her, holding her gaze, apparently no longer worried she may be uncomfortable. "You brought some with you."

"Yes, I… kind of got used to it. So…" She racked her brain trying to think of something impersonal to talk about. "How did the negotiations end up? Was Aurus happy with their end of the deal?"

"Very. They got the money they wanted and we got the land back. You helped us a great deal, Cara."

She looked up at him in surprise. "Helped?" she repeated faintly. "I thought—"

"What did you think?"

But with his heated gaze on her, all thought disappeared. She swallowed and felt a blush rising up from her chest, neck, devouring her face with its tell-tale color. She cleared her throat. She tore her eyes from his and walked into the tiny galley kitchen. "Are you hungry?" She picked up a pan and moved it to the bench, shifted crockery, open the larder door, as if looking for something, trying to hide her utter confusion. She picked out a loaf of bread. "There's a fantastic bakery downstairs. My friend runs it and keeps me supplied—"

She turned suddenly to find Tariq close behind her, his body filling the small space between her and the kitchen door.

"I'm not here for food, Cara."

"Oh… Well… it's nearly dinner time…I just thought…"

"Tell me, what *did* you think? Because it cannot be such a mystery, surely?"

She plucked a bread knife from the block and began slicing bread, very badly. "It certainly *is* a mystery. After you tell someone they're a 'traitor' and that you never want to see them again, surely it's not surprising I didn't expect to see you."

He shrugged. "Put it like that, I suppose, it's understandable."

She cut a swathe through the butter with a knife and spread it thickly onto the uneven bread, followed by a thick dollop from the nearest jar—marmite—topped with another doorstep of bread.

"That looks the most unappetizing sandwich I've ever seen. Is that what passes for dinner in your country?"

"I'm hungry." She brought it to her lips, but hesitated. "Or I was."

"Cara." He touched her arm and she stilled, the sandwich paused in mid-air, as ripples of delicious chills swept her body just from those fingers on her arm. She dropped the sandwich on the plate. "Tariq, I can't deal with this! You told me to go. You called me untrustworthy, deceitful—all true."

"It's also not surprising I said those things, under the circumstances. But nothing's ever as it seems, is it, Cara?" He picked up a family photograph. "Take this photograph, for instance. Your family, I presume?"

She nodded, unable to say anything as the emotion swelled inside while the man she loved looked down at the image of her parents, for whom she still grieved.

"I've heard so little about your family. We spent all our time together on my territory, with *my* people, *my* family." He nodded and looked around and then back to her suddenly. "I was wrong. I made too many assumptions. I understood nothing of you and your life."

"Tariq… We had so little time to talk about anything. Let's face it, we hardly know each other at all."

He turned and his eyes blazed with an intensity that seared. "Is that what you believe?"

"It's fact, Tariq."

"Not all facts are true."

She shook her head. "You're talking in riddles."

"Am I? Here's a fact for you. My lover kept a secret from me, one she knew was important to me. Does that make her deceitful? Untrustworthy? Or simply pragmatic, sensible, knowing my likely reaction and its possible consequences?"

Still Cara didn't speak. His words were like a knife piercing and teasing the tender wound of her betrayal.

"So who's the person at fault, then? Surely not the woman? Surely"—he replaced the photograph onto the cabinet and faced her once more—"surely it would be the man who was so sure his lover was an open book, a woman with no history—a woman whose past he'd made no attempt to discover? Hmm?"

Her mouth was dry, parched. She tried to speak but no sound came.

"I decided to remedy my lack of knowledge about you. After you left I began to research your family, to find out the facts, as much for me as to justify my actions. But when I discovered the facts, I found *my* actions couldn't be justified. Here, in this photograph, is your father, mother, you and your *ex*-husband." She noticed the emphasis on 'ex'. So he'd discovered she was now divorced. She nodded again. "A happy family photograph on the surface. But underneath?"

"How would you know what was behind that photograph?"

"I made it my business to know." He pointed to her father, standing tall, pale and gaunt-looking. "Your father must have had renal failure about the time the photograph was taken. You're smiling at the camera but I can see the pain in your eyes."

She leaned back against the kitchen cupboard. "I was desperate," she whispered as the memories flooded back.

"And there's your ex-husband, taking advantage of a sick man and a worried daughter by 'helping' him in his work.

Until he discovered what he needed after which he just left, didn't he?"

She gripped the bench, feeling suddenly weak. "Yes."

"I should have trusted you, but I didn't. If there's one thing you taught me, Cara, it's to understand the truth through my own senses. When I look into your eyes, when I listen to your voice, when I touch your skin, I know you better than any fact can tell me."

"And what do your senses say now about me?"

He stroked her arms that were held defensively in front of her. "That you're scared to open up, to believe in me again."

She nodded, once briefly. "What else?"

"That this is your only fear now. You've overcome your fear of loneliness, of grief, of the rain. You're stronger through your pain. But, Cara, I would take that last fear away from your eyes."

"And how would you propose to do that?"

"Come home with me. Back to Ma'in."

"Come back with you? To Ma'in?" She repeated his words, trying to make them real. But from the way his eyes darkened, she must have sounded more doubtful than wondering.

"Don't you understand? I can think of nothing, no one but you." He put his other hand on her arm. "In the morning I wake up with your image in my mind, the feeling of your body like an imprint against my skin." He squeezed her flesh, she knew he did, but all she felt was the pressure of his eyes burning into hers. He swallowed as if trying to control his words. "And at night." He shook his head. "At night it's the worst. Because I think I can sleep, I can rid myself of my need for you, but then I sleep and I cannot control my thoughts… or my body. *Cara*…" There it was again, the whisper like a prayer. "I can't live without you. I love you, with my whole being—my heart, my senses, my body, my mind. Every part of me yearns to be with you. *Cara*, I'm asking you to marry me, to become my wife, to live with me, to love me as I love you. I don't want to take anything from you, I only want to add to your life."

Dumbstruck, all she could do was stare. No thoughts, no words emerged. Fear entered his eyes.

"Cara! I'd do anything for you. We can keep a house here, if you wish. Live here part-time if it means so much to you."

Cara laughed. The thought of this King, living in an apartment in rural Norfolk was just too ridiculous. "I can't see that!"

He gripped her arms and the laughter fled.

"Seriously, you're King, you need to live in your country."

"My brother can share control of Ma'in."

"You'd give up your country?"

"I've lived my life for my country and now it's time to live my life for me. Me, you and my children. *Our* family. That's all I want now. That's all that's important."

"Tariq, I don't want you to give up what means so much to you."

"But you said this is your favorite place on earth." He looked down at her fisted hands and fiddled with her fingers.

"That might be what I said, but it wasn't what I meant."

He tilted her chin so he could see her eyes better. "What is it you meant, Cara?"

She had no choice but to look into his hot, questioning eyes. "I said this is my favorite place on earth. But I didn't say it was my home. *That* is something different. There is no species of tree, no design of house, no landscape, no weather, that defines my home."

He frowned. "What do you mean?"

"My home is wherever the people I love are, the people who love me. I couldn't come to be with you unless you wanted me as much as I want you. That's no life. But if you love me, then anything is possible. I can live anywhere now—rain, sun, mountains, city—so long as I'm with the person I love, who loves me. Tariq, wherever *you* are, is my home."

His eyes closed and the tension fell away. He pulled her to him and gently kissed the top of her head, before wrapping his arms around her.

Enfolded in his arms she knew the strength of his feeling, as well as the truth of her words—she'd found her home in his arms.

EPILOGUE

Three months later...

If it hadn't been for Tariq's hand holding hers tightly, Cara didn't know if she'd have got through the wedding ceremony. All her life she'd passed quietly through events and here she was, the center of attention, married to the King of Ma'in. She was Queen of Ma'in and realized that she'd never have the luxury of anonymity again.

Not that she wanted it, she thought to herself, as Tariq turned away from one of his guests and caught her eye. She was always at the forefront of his thoughts and attentions, and there was no way in this world that she wanted that to be any different.

It was late in the evening now. And the torches that lit the vast hall of Qusayr Zarqa revealed the heat in Tariq's expression. He wanted her. Just as he wanted her every night, and every day. She couldn't wait until they were alone. But she had to wait. Although some of their guests had retired for the night, their closest friends and family remained, listening to the music that was quieter now everyone was tired and the dancing had stopped.

"No regrets?" said Anna in a low voice. "It's a big thing taking on not just a sheikh, but a country, and a family, too."

"Not such a big thing," Cara replied. "With Tariq by my side."

Tariq was talking to Lucy who sat to his left, and hadn't heard the exchange but he drew Cara to his side in a brief hug. Anna noticed and grinned at Cara.

"Looks like he never intends to leave it too."

Cara placed her hand protectively over his. "He'd better not."

"He'd better not what?" Lucy called across to her.

"Lucy! You've ears like a bat!" laughed Anna.

"What? Tall and pointy?"

Tariq ignored the laughter which attracted Razeen and Zahir into the conversation and which soon veered off at a tangent, leaving Tariq and Cara in their own world, which was just how they liked it.

Tariq brushed his lips against Cara's ear. "And, what my darling, had I better not do?"

She shivered under his caress and turned to him with narrowed eyes. "And why do you assume I'm talking about you?"

"Who else would you talk of on your wedding night?"

"Maybe your brothers?"

Tariq followed her gaze first to Daidan, who sat aloof from the rest of them, dark and brooding, obviously biding time until he, too, could leave. "And what would you be saying about Daidan?"

"That if his thoughts are as dangerous as they appear, he'd better not act on them."

Tariq nodded. "Sound advice, given his marital status." He

turned and nodded toward Sahmir. "And my youngest brother? What would it be better that he didn't do?"

Cara looked across at Sahmir who sat, uncharacteristically quiet and thoughtful.

"Ah, with Sahmir I wouldn't tell him *not* do something. I'd tell him that he needed to act, now. He's not happy."

"Um, I think you're right."

"Did you ever discover the circumstances in which Sahmir and Rory got together?"

Tariq looked grim and shook his head. "No. He's not saying, which worries me. Sahmir has always told me everything. But not this time. No doubt I'll find out at some point. So that brings me back to me. What, my darling, had *I* better not do?"

She brought his hand to her stomach, slightly rounded now. "You'd better not leave us."

For a moment she thought Tariq hadn't understood. He began to reply and stopped as he suddenly understood.

"Us…" He fanned his fingers over her stomach, caressing her newly emerging curves. "You're…" He swallowed as if hardly daring to say the words out loud.

She laughed and nodded. "Pregnant. Yes. So you'd better not leave me."

He kissed her cheek, her hair and then her lips. "Never. You have me for life."

Cara sighed in sheer and utter contentment and gave herself up to the bliss of his kiss.

∼

AFTERWORD

Thank you for reading *Awakened by the Sheikh*. I hope you enjoyed it! Reviews are always welcome—they help me, and they help prospective readers to decide if they'd enjoy the book.

The Desert Kings series comprises:

> Wanted: A Wife for the Sheikh
> The Sheikh's Bargain Bride
> The Sheikh's Lost Lover
> Awakened by the Sheikh
> Claimed by the Sheikh
> Wanted: A Baby the the Sheikh

The next book in the Desert Kings series features Sahmir and Rory in *Claimed by the Sheikh* (excerpt follows). Here's a review of *Claimed by the Sheikh* to give you a taste of what to expect.

"Loved this alpha sheikh! He knows how to tempt a woman but also

AFTERWORD

how to respect her. You know he is a good man by what he does even though he has made some mistakes. He is determined to make things right!" (Patti A, Amazon.com)

You can check out all my books on the following pages. And, if you'd like to know when my next book is available, you can sign up for my new release e-mail list via my website —www.dianafraser.com.

Happy reading!

Diana

~

CLAIMED BY THE SHEIKH

BOOK 5 OF DESERT KINGS—SAHMIR AND RORY

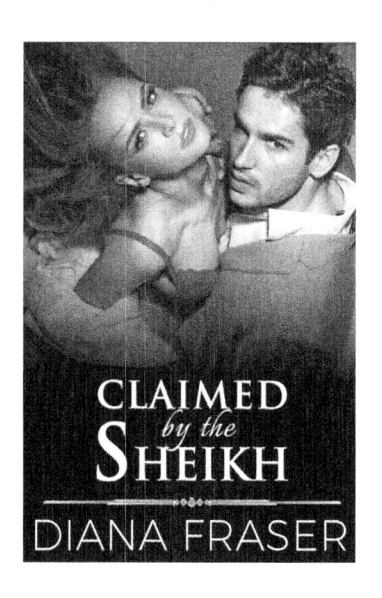

With an arranged, love-free marriage looming, Prince Sahmir of Ma'in is enjoying his last night in Paris when Aurora runs by, fleeing for her life. All Rory wants is to regain the estates her father lost to the Russian mafia. She hadn't planned on marrying the

Russian, or living with a sheikh and she certainly hadn't planned on a baby.

Excerpt

It was past midnight and the only sounds in the Place des Vosges were the lonely notes of Debussy that drifted through the open door, down to the steps where Prince Sahmir ibn Saleh al-Fulan stood drinking red wine and watching the snow fall.

He couldn't remember the last time he'd stopped to watch snow fall. Klosters maybe? Pre-teen definitely. Like intricate pieces of frozen coral, the snowflakes drifted down from the night sky in a lazy path, past the grey slate roof, and brick and stone striped façade of his Paris home, before coming to rest on the glossy pavement. As insubstantial as they were, they were beginning to accumulate, lightening the square to a world of white.

Sahmir narrowed his eyes against the glare. He'd spent too much time in heavily curtained hotel rooms—gambling by night and trying to forget his past in the arms of women by day. Too much darkness, too little light.

He let one flake settle on his hand and remembered how snow had fascinated him as a boy when he and his mother had left the heat of Ma'in for their annual holiday in Switzerland. He felt a flicker of that memory now, as he examined the white snowflake, momentarily perfect against his dark skin. He'd used to believe in magic, in fairytales. Where had that innocence gone?

The flake melted. He sighed, took another sip of red wine and looked across at the park where the snow was beginning to create shapes in the dark trees. He wouldn't be seeing snow again for a while. He'd done what he came to Paris to do. Now it was time to return to Ma'in, back to the responsibility he'd promised his dead sister he'd embrace.

Suddenly the sharp, urgent sound of stiletto heels unevenly stabbing the pavement came to him through the muffled, still air. He looked round to see a woman running along the street towards him. From the light of a street lamp he could see that she was tall and slender with long, dark hair that streamed behind her and she was wearing a bright red ball gown with a black bodice. No coat, despite the weather.

He could tell from the way she kept darting looks behind her that she was running from something or someone. And whoever that was had obviously put the fear of God—or the Devil—into her.

Don't get involved, the quiet voice of his sister whispered in his head.

He frowned, warring with the gentle voice that was the only thing which lay between him and trouble.

Don't get involved, it repeated. *Look what happened last time.*

As she drew level with him she turned to look behind her again and it was then that he knew he couldn't *not* get involved. Her eyes were wide with fear, but it was the vulnerability he saw there that shot straight to the core of him.

He barely felt his half-empty glass slip from his fingers as he pushed himself away from the wall and leaped down the steps and into the square after her. Whoever she was, wherever she'd come from, she needed help.

Buy Now!

∽

ALSO BY DIANA FRASER

The Mackenzies
The Real Thing
The PA's Revenge
The Marriage Trap
The Cowboy's Craving
The Playboy's Redemption
The Lakehouse Café

New Zealand Brides
Yours to Give
Yours to Treasure
Yours to Cherish

Desert Kings
Wanted: A Wife for the Sheikh
The Sheikh's Bargain Bride
The Sheikh's Lost Lover
Awakened by the Sheikh
Claimed by the Sheikh
Wanted: A Baby by the Sheikh

Italian Romance
Perfect
Her Retreat
Trusting Him
An Accidental Christmas

Printed in Great Britain
by Amazon